Slocum had trailed them now across a thousand miles, relentless, driven, his every thought bent to that one task, riding from daybreak till dark with sometimes nothing but hate to fill his belly, always watching the farthest dot on the horizon hoping it might be them, scouring every habitation he came to for the faintest scrap of news: a face remembered by a desk clerk in a dingy hotel, a name overheard in a wayside stage station, a horse described by strangers that matched a horse he'd seen before.

And now he had reached the end of the trail. They had gone to ground in Hobbs' Hole. All Slocum had to do now was find them.

And then watch their faces while they looked down the barrel of his gun.

He wanted to see fear in their eyes before he killed them.

## OTHER BOOKS BY JAKE LOGAN

# JAKE LOGAN

## GUNPLAY AT HOBBS' HOLE

BERKLEY BOOKS, NEW YORK

GUNPLAY AT HOBBS' HOLE

A Berkley Book / published by arrangement with
the author

PRINTING HISTORY
Berkley edition / May 1985

ISBN: 0-425-07683-0

A BERKLEY BOOK® TM 757,375
Berkley Books are published by The Berkley Publishing Group,
200 Madison Avenue, New York, N.Y. 10016.
The name "BERKLEY" and the stylized "B" with design are trademarks
belonging to Berkley Publishing Corporation.

PRINTED IN THE UNITED STATES OF AMERICA

# 1

Slocum laid his firearms on the crude table in the center of the room and wiped the last of the gun oil off his shotgun.

Rain drummed steadily on the roof, and a cold wind beat against the walls. The place was only a one-room shack set on a hillside—empty save for a broken mirror on one wall, the table, and two equally crude chairs—but he was glad just to have shelter. He'd found it by chance the day before, scouting the eastern rim of Hobbs' Hole, not wanting to ride on in without seeing what he would have at his back. The fire in the fireplace and the deerhide he'd tacked over the windows was all that kept the cold out, but he didn't plan on staying here long.

Only long enough to hunt down four men. The four men he'd been trailing since early August.

Hunt them down. Find out what he needed to know. And then kill them.

One by one if he could. All in a bunch if he had to.

Then maybe that ice that numbed his brain would melt and he would be able to feel again.

He broke the shotgun open and sighted through the breech. Two gleaming barrels, extra shiny where he'd worked with his bore brush just ahead of the chamber. It was a ten-gauge, a Greener goosegun with both barrels sawed off at eight inches. He didn't ordinarily carry it, but Hobbs' Hole was said to be populated solely by men on the dodge.

Going in alone against four men was risky enough. By now they might have joined up with more.

He took two shells of double-ought buck from a box on the table and rammed them into the breech. Then he clicked the Greener closed and picked up his Colt.

He thumbed the hammer back to half-cock and opened the loading gate. From another box he punched in five rounds, .45 caliber rimfire, turning the cylinder between thumb and middle finger. Then he closed the loading gate, eased the hammer down on the empty chamber, and slipped the Colt into the holster tied down on his thigh. When he'd fed fifteen rounds of .44 caliber into the magazine of his Winchester, he shouldered into his sheepskin and went outside.

Heavy black clouds had brought a misty twilight to what was actually noon, but the rain had slacked off to a drizzle. From the woodshed at the rear of the shack he took his saddle and gear and climbed through wet grass to where his horses stood head down in the apple orchard. While he saddled the bay, he scanned what little country he could see from here.

Smoke trickled up from the chimney at the back of the shack, but he figured he was safe enough. The road was five miles to the south and, as far as he could tell, these hills along the eastern rim of the Hole were deserted. Between him and the shack was a weathered outhouse, leaning with age, and near a corner of the orchard a jumbled pile of boards showed where a barn had collapsed. Whoever had home-steaded this unlikely place hadn't fared too well. He led the bay down for a drink at the rain barrel under the eaves and went back inside.

He hung the Greener by its sling across his chest, so that the shotgun rested butt-forward against his left hip, and buttoned his rain slicker on over his sheepskin. Then he threw another log on the fire to keep it going good, and crossed to the mirror near the door. Stuck down into the frame was the faded sepia photograph he'd spent a good hour brooding over the night before.

For weeks now he had done the same thing in every hotel he'd stopped in—fastened the picture to a wall and spent half the night brooding over it. By now he could conjure it up whole without even looking: himself and three friends posed in Saturday night finery for a cowtown photographer in front of a backdrop painted to look like sage. Charley Beaumont, bearded and runty and grinning like a fool, one boot propped on a chair so he could display both sixgun and Winchester across his knee; Bob Foley, tall and cool and showing that charm that always drew women to him; and Paul Quinn, "Pablito" when he was drunk, bright-eyed and jaunty, wearing wooly chaps and a cartridge belt across his chest, his shiny black hair cropped short because he figured that way nobody could tell he was half-Greaser.

And himself beside Quinn, the only one not smiling, his Winchester in the crook of his arm. At the start of a spree after a long trail drive from Texas, wanting a picture to sport for the girls in the saloons.

They had had a fine time that night, if he remembered it right. They'd had a lot of fine times together. His best friends once—the men in that picture.

He had trailed them now across a thousand miles,

relentless, driven, his every thought bent to that one task, riding from daybreak till dark with sometimes nothing but hate to fill his belly, always watching the farthest dot on the horizon hoping it might be them, scouring every habitation he came to for the faintest scrap of news: a face remembered by a desk clerk in a dingy hotel, a name overheard in a wayside stage station, a horse described by strangers that matched a horse he'd seen before.

Now he had reached the end of the trail. They had gone to ground in Hobbs' Hole. All he had to do now was find them.

Them and Frank Walker, the man they had thrown in with, a man he didn't know well enough even to recognize. Find them and brace them and drag out of them the truth about what they had done.

And then watch their faces while they looked down the barrel of his gun.

He wanted to see fear in their eyes before he killed them.

From the mirror his own eyes gazed back at him, opaque green flames behind which even he could not see, with that bronze glint in them which had once led a man to declare Slocum mad. The man had been wrong—or partly wrong—but he hadn't lived long enough to learn his error.

The sound of the rain on the roof had ceased. He plucked the picture from the mirror and slipped it into his slicker pocket. Then he left the shack, mounted up, and started down through the hills toward the road.

# 2

Four miles west along the road he halted the bay at the edge of Hobbs' Hole, a flat expanse of grassland ringed by mountains. It looked ten miles square, the black sky locked down on it like a lid. Two miles to the south he saw the lights of a single low building. That would be Bushnell's, the saloon and store he'd heard about, the only trace of civilization for more than ninety miles. Anybody hiding out here would have to come into Bushnell's sooner or later.

He flicked the spurs and eased the bay down the muddy road into the Hole.

When he got close he saw that Bushnell's was made of log, a one-story structure with a sod roof and separate doors leading into store and saloon. The store on the right was dark; the saloon window on the left showed warm yellow light. The hitching rail was empty, but likely the barn out back was where a man stabled his mount in weather like this. He circled around to dismount at the rear of the barn and led the bay in through a set of tall double doors.

The smell of manure and stale hay was strong inside. He could hear the sound of his own breathing and the rustle of his slicker skirts as he loosed the buttons to get at the shotgun. He tied the bay to a stanchion and slipped into the first of the stalls, talking softly to soothe the horse while he felt along its flank for the brand.

Working quickly, checking horses and gear, he went through all ten stalls before he found what he was looking for: a black-tailed dun with a Lazy J brand. He crouched in the straw, trying to hold himself in check, feeling the heat beating at the back of his eyes. The Lazy J was where Frank Walker had been working when the others signed on there, back in Texas, in Jackson County. He thought of Anne in that house back there and himself coming home to find her lying in her own blood, muddy bootprints on the floor around the tub she'd been taking a bath in, her hands still clutching the knife in her belly. Some murderous rage tried to struggle free of the ice that numbed his brain, and he worked hard to get it back under control. Numbness seemed the only thing keeping him sane.

He forced himself to think. From the look of things, Walker was here alone. And far as he knew, the man had never laid eyes on him. He had never laid eyes on Walker, either, but he had one advantage. He'd been told the man had a rope scar on his neck. Getting the neckerchief off for a look might be a little chancy, but that was why he'd brought the Greener. A man could be pretty persuasive with a scattergun. He rose from his crouch and slipped out through the front doors.

The windows at the rear of the store were curtained; likely Bushnell's living quarters were in there. Through the windows in back of the saloon he saw a black man in a cook's hat moving around in a kitchen. Circling wide left through wet grass, he came around in front of the store and mounted onto the porch. Careful to set his boots down quiet on the planking, he eased past the dark window and the store entrance to where he could lay an ear up against the saloon door. He listened until he was sure there was nobody waiting behind it. Then he turned the latch and stepped inside.

The sound of the door cut the hum of talk off sharp. He could see heads turned his way all over the room. The place was narrow and low-ceilinged, with three oilcloth-covered tables spaced out along the left wall and a bar running halfway down on the right. Through the smoke in the air he counted six men besides the barkeep, all at the tables, but he didn't recognize a one. Warily, he moved down the bar to where he could watch them in the back bar mirror.

"Whiskey."

The barkeep, likely Bushnell himself, came to pour him a glass. Beefy and short, with a head like a hog's, he eyed Slocum through lashes so pale he seemed to have none at all. "Ain't seen you in here before," he said.

"Ain't been in here before."

Slocum tasted the whiskey, watching the mirror. The murmur of talk had swelled up again from a card game at a table in the rear. A lean man with cool gray eyes and a dark moustache was watching him over a drink from the table nearest the window. Slocum met his eyes and the man glanced away, but he didn't look to be a man who backed down easy. A redheaded man was eating alone at the center table, his back to the room. Two of the men in the card game had their backs to the room as well; the other two were keeping an eye on him over their cards.

Now from behind a thin partition came the clash of pots and pans in the kitchen, and he suddenly realized he was hungry. "I could use a meal. What's on the menu?"

"What's always on the menu," Bushnell said, and nodded toward a signboard tacked above the kitchen door: *T-bone, potatoes, apple pie & coffee—50 cents*.

"I'll have it," Slocum said.

A short, hefty woman, likely Bushnell's wife, had come to lean against the jamb of a curtained-off doorway into the store. Bushnell gave her a nod and she went back into the kitchen. Slocum sipped at his whiskey and scanned the tables in the mirror.

Nobody seemed to be paying him any mind, but he knew that was deceptive. Any stranger coming in here could be the law or a bounty hunter, and likely every man here had reason to fear either. Walker, knowing what he had done, knowing Slocum was on his trail, would have special cause to fear any man he didn't know. And any one of the six could be Walker. It struck him suddenly that one of them *had* to be Walker, and he felt something mean and reckless rise up inside him. The thought that Walker was in this room was suddenly more than he could stand. Likely it wasn't smart, but watching Bushnell eye him from under the back bar mirror he had a sudden urge to bring the whole thing to a head right here.

"My name's Slocum," he said to Bushnell, loud enough for everybody to hear. "John Slocum. I'm looking for a man named Frank Walker. Frank Walker, and his friends. You know a man around here by the name of Frank Walker?"

Bushnell had his hands tucked up under the bib of his apron. He didn't blink an eye. "No, I don't. I wouldn't say so if I did."

"Used to work for the Lazy J down in Jackson County, Texas." Slocum downed his whiskey and slid the glass across the bar. "Maybe some of your friends know him."

"You come to the wrong place," Bushnell said.

"I'm in the right place. I'll find the right man, too."

He was keeping his eyes on the mirror. Nothing had changed, nobody had moved, and that disappointed him. One of them had to be Walker. That lean man at the front table, for instance, with the dark moustache and the cool gray eyes, was having a hard time hiding his interest in the conversation at the bar. That heat flared up behind Slocum's eyes again, and he wanted to sling his glass at the mirror just to get their attention.

"Your dinner, sir."

He turned to see a dark-haired young woman at his elbow, holding a plate of food in one hand and a napkin-wrapped knife and fork in the other. The sight of her made his blood jump. She was barely tall enough to reach his shoulder, her waist was so slim he could have circled it with his hands, but her breasts were big enough for a woman twice her size. She was so astonishingly voluptuous he could tell she was resigned to being stared at by every man she met.

She nodded at the plate, trying to ignore where his eyes were. "Will you want it here at the bar, sir, or shall I take it to a table?"

Ever since he'd found Anne dead, wanting a woman had put a strange queasiness in his belly, almost like he hated the woman who was making him want her. Not a pleasant feeling. To escape it now, he took the plate and the utensils from her. "I'll eat at a table," he said, and turned away from the bar.

He straddled a spare chair at the table where the redhead was, putting his back to the wall, the shotgun under his slicker bumping against the chair leg. The redhead, finished with his meal, was digging for something in his vest pocket. He flashed Slocum a look.

"The table's taken."

"Looks clear to me," Slocum said. "You pay rent on it?"

He was alert and aware of every man in the room, but he didn't think this one was Walker. He remembered hearing that Walker was over thirty, and this man was barely twenty-one. But there was a mean look showing through those boyish freckles and something strange about the cheekbones, like maybe they'd been honed sharp below eyes keen and eager for trouble.

The redhead fished a toothpick from a vest pocket and stuck it between his teeth. "Looking for a man named Frank Walker, are you?"

"That's what I said. Walker or any of the three he's riding with. Charley Beaumont, Paul Quinn, Bob Foley. You know them?"

The redhead grinned, and the grin made him look like a boy again. "I'll say one thing for you. You got guts. Man don't just walk into Hobbs' Hole and say right out he's hunting bounty. Or whatever it is you're doing."

"What I'm doing is my business. I'd be obliged if you'd tend to your own."

The redhead cocked his head, the toothpick at a jaunty angle between his teeth. "Maybe I am. Maybe my business is taking care of strangers nosing around in the Hole."

"You better tend to your schoolwork, sonny. I'm in no mood for play."

The redhead lost his grin, and a deep flush rose up under his freckles. He took the toothpick out of his mouth and gazed at Slocum, something smoky and dangerous just behind his eyes. "Don't nobody talk to me like that," he said. "For sure not in the Hole. Maybe you'd best leave while you're still walking."

"I hurt your feelings?" Slocum said. "I apologize."

He wondered which one of the others was Walker, and if the redhead and Walker were together. The redhead was for sure trying to provoke trouble. Could be he was setting up a play for Walker. That was all right. That would flush Walker out. One look at that shotgun, and Walker would get real sensible. Then they would go find the others.

He was watching the redhead pat down his pockets when something moved at his elbow and he found the woman setting a cup of coffee beside his plate. He couldn't help looking at her—a womanly girl in a coarse, patched dress, wearing a man's heavy shoes and a length of rope for a belt, but none of it hiding that astonishing body. Avoiding his eyes, she edged around the table to gather up the redhead's dishes, those remarkable breasts jostling and jiggling as she moved.

The redhead was watching him, his grin back, and the toothpick stuck back in the grin. "She's a sight for a hungry man's eyes, ain't she? Bushnell hired her on to keep the rest of us coming in here." He reached out and patted her ass.

She flushed and swivelled away from his hand, trying to ignore him while she stacked his dishes on her arm.

"Susan, honey, fetch me my makings. My sheep-skin's hanging on that peg back there," the redhead ordered.

The girl flushed again, stricken eyes suddenly locked

on Slocum's. Then the redhead grinned and she hurried away toward the kitchen.

"Bring me some more of that coffee," the redhead called after her, and got up to fish in the pockets of the sheepskin hanging on the wall.

Slocum forced his mind back to his steak. His throat was so tight he could barely get enough breath. Knowing what had likely happened to Anne before she died, he couldn't tolerate seeing a man even touching a woman against her will.

When he had his voice under control, he said, "Where I come from, we'd hang a man for laying hands on a woman like that."

"Why'n't you go back there, then?" The redhead had his makings out now and was building himself a smoke. "We don't like strangers here. Especially strangers asking questions."

The girl came back then, carrying a coffee pot. She had to move around between the redhead and the table to get at his cup, and Slocum could see it made her nervous, bending over with her back to the man like that.

The redhead flashed that deceptively boyish grin at Slocum. "You made a new friend here, Susan. Man says he don't like me touching you." He leaned down to cup her left breast, watching Slocum with those sharp eyes. "You don't mind that, now, do you, Susan, honey?"

The girl flushed, almost spilling the coffee. Shamefaced, she twisted loose from the redhead's grasp and hurried for the kitchen.

Slocum waited till she was ten steps away. Then he reared back and kicked the table over.

He was on his feet before the noise subsided. He

had the Greener pointing at the card game and his
Colt out holding on the man at the front table, and
just the sight of his face halted Bushnell halfway toward what was likely a shotgun under the bar.

Even he could hear the cold menace in his voice:
"Everybody freeze. Anybody moves, I'll put blood
all over the walls."

The men at the card game were halfway to their
feet. The redhead was swearing and struggling on the
floor, half under the table, all tangled up in the oilcloth
and fighting to get it off him. Bushnell was still half
bent over just back of the bar, but he had his hands
in the air and his eyes on the Greener. Only that lean
man at the front table had stayed where he was, hands
laid carefully on the table-top to show he wasn't trying
anything.

"Fine. Stay like that." Slocum turned the Colt on
that frantic shape under the oilcloth. "Come out of
there empty-handed, Red, or you'll die when you do."

"You're asking for trouble, stranger," Bushnell said.

Slocum turned on him, feeling that heat flare up
inside. "I'm not asking for trouble, I'm giving it out.
You want some, I'll be glad to oblige."

"There's rules here. You can't do this in here."

"I'm changing the rules. Get away from that shotgun and come out from behind the bar."

The redhead had got the oilcloth off and was on
his knees, but the sight of Slocum's sixgun kept him
there. That smoky look was back in his eyes. "You're
a dead man, friend. You're still walking around, but
you're a dead man. Nobody causes trouble in the
Hole."

"Shut up." Slocum waved the Greener at the men
from the card game. "You. I want you out here where

I can see you. One at a time."

The redhead was still on his knees. "You're a stranger here, friend. I'll give you fair warning. I'm David Hobbs. You don't pull something like this with me."

"Shut up." Slocum waved the Greener at the rear table. "Come on. Step out front to the bar. Drop your gunbelts and sit on the floor where I can see you plain. Sit on your hands, so I won't get nervous with this thing." He waved the Colt at Bushnell. "That goes for you, too. Lift that shotgun out of there real careful and bring it out here and lay it on the floor. Then you sit with the rest."

Bushnell gingerly brought the shotgun up, holding it by the muzzle, and edged out from behind the bar. One by one, carefully watching the Greener, the men from the card game came out along the bar and did as they were told. Slocum studied each one as they dropped their gunbelts, looking for signs they might know who he was, might be scared he knew who they were. Only one of them looked like he could be Walker—a sullen-looking gent in a fancy red shirt. When the last of them was sitting on the floor, the gray-eyed man with the dark moustache moved cautiously from the front table to do the same. Then Slocum waved his Colt at the redhead.

"You, too."

The redhead looked at the Greener and stifled whatever it was he was itching to do. "This is Hobbs' Hole you're in," he said. "Walter Hobbs is a man nobody messes with. He finds out what you're pulling in the Hole, you won't live to get out of it." But he got to his feet, carefully deposited his gunbelt on the pile, and joined the rank along the front of the bar.

The girl had fled into the kitchen. Bushnell's wife was clinging wide-eyed to the doorjamb. The cook might have a gun in the kitchen, but Slocum figured a black would have no loyalty to a man like Bushnell. Slocum waved the Colt at the gray-eyed man with the dark moustache, the one who'd been at the front table.

"You. Take your neckerchief off and open your collar. I want to look at your neck."

The man was sitting casually on his hands, leaning back against the front of the bar like the others. Now he raised his eyebrows in surprise, but he didn't protest. Carefully he brought his hands out and unknotted his kerchief. When he had the kerchief off, he unbuttoned his collar and spread it wide. Holding the Greener on the others, Slocum looked just long enough to see there was no scar on the man's neck. The heat of anger rose up in him again.

From his place on the floor along the bar, the redhead said, "Better quit while you're ahead, friend."

"Shut up." Slocum moved to put the shotgun on the other man that fit Walker's description—the sullen man from the card game, in the fancy red shirt. "Now you. Take your kerchief off and spread your collar."

The man gave him a look of pure hate, but he did as he was told. There was no scar on his neck, either.

Slocum spun on his heel and moved back to where he could put the shotgun on them all. "I want a look at everybody. One of you's got a scar on his neck. Ain't none of the rest of you got cause to worry. Take 'em off. One at a time."

"You can play your shirt-collar game all day," the redhead said. "You'll find we don't play in the Hole."

Slocum ignored him. While each man loosed the

kerchief from around his neck, he moved along the row to get a look at them all. One by one each kerchief came off and was tossed aside. One by one each man opened his collar. When he reached the end of the row, he still hadn't found a scar.

Angry, he turned to stride along the row. "Who owns that black-tailed dun in the stable? The dun with the Lazy J brand?" He stopped in the center of the room and scanned the row of faces. Nobody was looking at him. "I'm looking for the man that owns the dun. I got nothing against anybody else. I want to know who owns that horse."

Nobody answered. He started pacing along the bar, watching faces. "I got to blow somebody's foot off to get an answer, I'll do it. I'm looking for four men. One of them has a rope scar on his neck. Last I heard he was riding that dun. He ain't in here. I want to know where he is."

"I own the dun," Bushnell said.

Slocum looked at him. "You? Where'd you get a Lazy J horse?"

"Bought it off a man passing through here. Said he needed the money. Traded him a six-year-old mare and paid him twenty extra. I got a good deal."

"Maybe you did. And maybe you were helping a friend shed something from his past. But let's say he was passing through. Where'd he go when he left here?"

"I got no idea."

"Was he alone? He have anybody with him?"

"I don't remember seeing."

"He say what his name was?"

"I didn't ask."

Slocum holstered his Colt. "You're a real fund of

information, ain't you?" From an inside pocket he took the picture he'd brought from the shack and held it down in front of Bushnell's face. "You ever seen any of these men? Other than the one that's me? Think hard on it. You say no and I find out you have, I might take a real dislike to you."

Bushnell eyed the picture and then looked away. "I never seen none of them."

Slocum stuck the picture in front of the man in the red shirt. "How about you. You seen any of 'em around here?"

The man shook his head, but he wouldn't meet Slocum's eyes. They would none of them talk, even if they knew anything to say, but his anger wouldn't let him stop. He showed the picture to the next man and got the same answer, moved to the next and got the same answer there, the heat building in him with every sullen refusal he met. Methodically, he asked each man the same questions and one by one each man gave him the same answer, and when he reached the end of the row he turned on his heel looking for somebody else, because his anger was starting to put him out of control.

"I ought to warn you," Bushnell said. "Lawmen don't survive long around here."

"I'm not a lawman." He put the picture away and drew his Colt again. "You." He pointed to the man with the gray eyes. "Take that oilcloth off the floor and put those gunbelts in it. Careful-like, else this shotgun might go off."

While the man moved to do as he was told, Slocum paced along the bar, giving each man a good look at the muzzle of that Greener. "Just so you know the score. Those were friends of mine in that picture. Used to be friends of mine. They killed a woman down in Texas. A woman that meant a lot to me. Raped her and killed her and left her naked on the floor for me to come home and find. I've trailed them across a thousand miles of country. If I have to, I'll trail them a thousand miles more. But I know they're somewhere in the Hole. Next time you see 'em, you tell 'em John Slocum's here. Tell 'em I'll hunt 'em till I find 'em. Tell 'em I won't rest till I see every one of 'em dead. You got that?"

Nobody answered.

Slocum kicked Bushnell. "You got that?"

"I got it," Bushnell said.

"Good."

The gray-eyed man had collected the gunbelts in the oilcloth, which he held now like a sack. Slocum backed over beside him, keeping his shotgun on the men along the bar, and put his Colt up under the man's nose.

"The rest of you just sit tight," he said. "The two of us are going outside. I'll leave your weapons in the stable. You can get 'em after I'm gone."

He backed out onto the porch, the other man carrying the oilcloth and keeping pace alongside him. On the porch, he holstered his Colt and held out his hand for the oilcloth.

The other man gave it to him. Quietly, too low for the others to hear, he said, "Listen close, but don't let on I'm talking. Man named Tom Price lives in a shack down at the southeast corner of the Hole. Meet me there in about four hours. Name's Will Ganning. Maybe I can help you."

Surprised, Slocum looked at him. He saw again what had struck him the first time he'd seen the man:

a look of cool self-assurance, the lean face expressionless behind the dark moustache, and nothing in those gray eyes to give away what he was thinking.

"Careful around the redhead," Ganning said. "He's one of Walter Hobbs' sons. Hobbs runs things here in the Hole." Then, holding his hands out away from his sides, he backed away till his boot heel struck the doorjamb behind him. He turned then to slip through the door sideways, leaving Slocum a look at the men still sitting on their hands along the wall.

Carrying the oilcloth in one hand, Slocum skirted quickly around the store. In the barn he dumped the gunbelts in a trough, untied the bay, and mounted up. He rode out the rear doors and headed straight south across the Hole, spurring the bay into a gallop.

# 3

When he reached the south edge of the Hole he burst on up through a little screen of willows onto a trail running east and west along the base of the hills. Once inside the trees, he reined up and turned to look back the way he had come. Bushnell's was a black hulk in the misty drizzle, maybe three miles away. He wasn't surprised to see a rider crossing the flat from Bushnell's toward the hills along the eastern rim of the Hole.

He dug a pair of field glasses out of his saddlebags and slowly brought the rider into focus. Despite the drizzle and the dull light under those dark clouds he had no trouble making out David Hobbs hunched in the saddle, hat pulled down to keep the wet off his face. Hobbs was riding straight east, making no move toward the road. The Hole was narrower there, maybe a mile from Bushnell's to the rim, and Hobbs had already covered most of it. Slocum watched him trot on up the first little rise and disappear into the timber.

From searching the eastern rim the day before Slocum knew there was nothing there but empty hills and what was likely a stretch of this same trail angling off east to join the road. Hobbs wasn't heading for the road. He knew Hobbs' kind too well to believe that. Hobbs had marked where the bay had gone and was figuring to cut back fast around the rim. Likely he figured he was being watched and was making like he wasn't going anywhere special, but Slocum had no doubt he was aiming to settle scores.

He put the field glasses back in his saddlebags and pushed the bay on west, staying on the muddy trail so as to leave clear tracks. He had no plan as yet, but he was glad for the chance Hobbs was handing him. He needed a way to work off that heat inside.

After half a mile he happened on a shallow creek rushing down through the pines. He reined the bay off the trail into the creek and urged it uphill through the fast-running water. He had no idea where he was going, but that wasn't important now. Hobbs would be following his tracks, and what he wanted now was to keep Hobbs guessing.

Several hundred yards up into the timber, he came on a shelf of rock on the right where the creek had eaten the soil out from under the bank. He jumped the bay up onto the shelf and rode along the rock till it petered out. Then he sank in the spurs and felt the bay hunker on its hocks and leap for the dry ground. When he was a dozen yards up into the trees, he dismounted and came back to check the creek bank. He broke a branch off a pine tree and climbed back up the slope, sweeping the ground behind him as he went. When he was satisfied he'd left no trail, he swung back into the saddle and headed upstream again, staying just that dozen yards up from the creek bank.

When he neared the crest of the ridge he took his field glasses out again and scanned what he could see of the hills along the eastern rim of the Hole. He found the spot where he'd come up through the willows onto the trail, but there was no sign of Hobbs yet. He returned the field glasses to his saddlebags and reined the bay down the little slope and crossed the creek back east again.

On the far bank, he dismounted and dug a "Wanted" flyer out of his pocket and stuck it on the end of a little tree branch. He had been leaving flyers all the way from Texas, but he wouldn't be needing them anymore now. When he was satisfied the white of the flyer would catch the eye of anybody passing, he mounted up and headed back east along the crest of the ridge.

He rode another mile east before cutting back downhill. He left a flyer where he turned there, too, spearing it on the tip of a tree limb like he'd done with the first, face out and eye-level to a rider. He left another halfway down the ridge toward the trail, easing the bay down through the timber and watching the terrain ahead of him now. He would be coming in sight of the trail soon, and he wanted to see Hobbs before Hobbs saw him.

He was making no attempt to cover his tracks now. If Hobbs followed them this far, the man would know he was leaving trail on purpose. The question was, what would Hobbs do when he learned it.

When he'd left the last of his flyers on a tree just up the slope from the trail, he flicked his spurs and sent the bay on at a lope, then angling back around to a high knoll he had marked earlier. There was just enough timber on top of the knoll to shield him without blocking his view, and it gave him a look down the trail Hobbs should be taking. He brought his field glasses out again, settled himself in the saddle, and waited.

He didn't have to wait long. Hobbs had made good time. He was moving at a fast walk now, riding a black, coming along the trail from the east. Slocum was maybe a hundred yards up the ridge and just east of the spot where he himself had ridden up out of the Hole. Now he saw Hobbs come upon those tracks there and abruptly draw rein. The man whipped his head around, checking where the tracks came up through the willows screening the trail, then turned to scan the trail up ahead. He nodded to himself now and kicked his black in the flanks and started on at a trot.

Eager. Maybe too eager for his own good. He hadn't even tried to check his backtrail or what might be lurking in the timber off to the side. Keeping his field glasses out, Slocum nudged the bay in the flanks and started after him.

He stayed just far enough back to keep out of sight and not lose the black in the trees. He wasn't sure himself what his aim was, but he figured trailing Hobbs was worth the effort, if only to teach the man it wouldn't do to try settling the score he had in mind settling. And maybe Hobbs knew where Walker and the others were. If his daddy ran things here in the Hole, the way Ganning said, it figured anybody coming to roost here would make himself known to Hobbs. And what Hobbs knew, maybe his sons knew, too.

When he reached the creek, Hobbs didn't hesitate long. He circled around the opposite bank till he was sure the tracks didn't continue on. Then he cut a glance down through the willows toward the Hole and another up the creek. He gave it maybe twenty seconds' thought and sent the black lunging up the far side of the stream.

He was a little more alert now, watching the trees up ahead, but he hadn't yet thought to check his backtrail. Slocum stayed on the near side of the creek, far enough back to keep Hobbs in sight but still give himself cover if Hobbs showed any signs of checking his rear.

He was pleased to see Hobbs ride past the rock shelf without noticing anything. If he'd been aiming to, he would have lost the man right there. Careless again. Knowing how careless a man was might come in handy some day. As it was, Hobbs noticed nothing out of the way till he reached the crest of the ridge, where the stream came bubbling out of a limestone cave. Then he saw the first of the flyers.

He splashed across the creek and plucked the flyer from its limb and looked at it close. That was when he started reining his horse around, looking sharp behind him and listening hard.

Slocum stayed out of sight in the trees, watching through the glasses. The flyer was a sketch he'd had done in Texas, from the picture he'd shown Hobbs in Bushnell's. Finding it hanging up here in the brush, Hobbs had to know he was being led on a goose chase.

He obviously didn't like the feeling that gave him. He threw the flyer away and found where the tracks went and spurred his horse after them, breaking into a trot now. Slocum hung back a ways, keeping the man in sight through the glasses. Seeing Hobbs scared pleased him. Teach the pup not to think so high of himself.

Hobbs didn't stop even to look at the second flyer. He reined left down the slope following those tracks, watching the trees on either side now. The ground was so steep there he had to pull up and ease his horse down slow.

Slocum marked where he figured the horse would come out. Then he stowed the field glasses and cut catty-corner down the slope himself, aiming to head

Hobbs off before he reached the trail.

He was waiting in the pines just above the trail when he heard the black coming down through the timber. He'd unlimbered his rope and shaken out a loop. He nudged the bay forward, toward the edge of the trees he was sheltering behind, holding the loop ready down along his thigh. He was already swinging it over his head when Hobbs came trotting past.

The rope caught Hobbs around the shoulders. He didn't see it coming, didn't hear a thing, didn't even have time to rein up. The rope yanked him out of the saddle, and the black kept right on going.

He landed on his back already kicking, letting out something halfway between a shout and a scream. Slocum vaulted from the saddle, hitting the ground at a run, unslinging his shotgun. Hobbs rolled up to his knees, and the rope went taut as the bay leaned against its pull and jerked him down again. Shouting, clawing for the Colt in his holster, Hobbs wriggled up again, and again the bay yanked him back down on his face.

Then Slocum was beside him. He stuck the muzzle of the shotgun in the back of the man's neck and reached down to lift the Colt from the holster still damp from Bushnell's trough. "That's a good Texas cow horse," he said, "used to pulling calves like you to the ground. Might as well stay where you are."

Hobbs was swearing. His face was in the dirt, but he'd stopped struggling, all his attention centered on that shotgun in the nape of his neck. Careful not to move, he spit the dirt out of his mouth and got some breath back.

"What the hell you doing? You just bought yourself a bullet, that's what y'did, y'bought yourself a bullet. Don't nobody treat a Hobbs like that and live."

Slocum stuck Hobbs' Colt in his belt and backed off a foot or two, keeping the Greener on him. "I might ask what you were doing, Red. Nobody asked you to come down here tracking me."

Hobbs spat out some more dirt. "Maybe you didn't hear who I am. The name is Hobbs. My old man runs this Hole. I make it my business to keep a watch on troublemakers that come into it."

"You ain't quite up to the job. You hadn't been so busy trying to count coup on me, you'd'a thought to check your backtrail a little closer. You aim to pursue your daddy's path, son, you got to smarten up a little. A thing like that'll get you killed."

"You let me up from here, and we'll see who it is gets killed."

"You see what I mean? That ain't a smart thing to say. Gives a man too much cause to see you don't get up. Maybe you better stick to your lessons till you're grown a little more, Red."

"Go to hell."

"I've no doubt that's where I'm headed, but it'll be without your help." Slocum grinned. "We'll have a fine reunion there. You and me and all your friends. Like Walker and those three with him. Where are they?"

"I told you. I got no idea. My daddy don't tell me everything he knows."

"I don't imagine he does, from the look of you. Wouldn't be smart. Still, you got ambition, don't you? Maybe you do a little snooping yourself. I'd be surprised, you don't know more than your daddy thinks you do."

"Maybe I do. It don't mean I know where your friends are."

*"Your* friends. Not mine anymore." Slocum watched Hobbs work his lips against his teeth. It was hard to talk with your mouth in the dirt. The man's black horse had circled back around and was standing over under a tree. "Tell you what I'm going to do, Red. Since you're not quite full-grown yet, I'm going to make an exception in your case. I generally don't let a man walk away that says he aims to kill me. In your case, I figure it's more talk than anything. You're lucky I do. I'm going to turn you loose, like I would any range calf not weaned yet. You go tell your daddy John Slocum's in the Hole and aims to stay till his job's done. Tell him what the job is. Tell him if he gets in my way, I'll see this place has cause for re-naming. I don't care who he is. You understand me?"

"Let me up. You got my gun. Let me up from here."

Slocum put the muzzle of the shotgun under Hobbs' chin and lifted the man's head up so he could see his eyes. "You tell your daddy that, the way I said."

Hobbs went nearly cross-eyed watching the shot-gun, but he tried to bluff it out. "I warned you. You're asking for trouble."

"Trouble's all I got. Got plenty to share. Looking for somebody to share it with. Your daddy wants to share it, tell him he's welcome. But tell him, too, I just want what any sane man would. You tell him what I said in Bushnell's. He's got any decency, he ought to understand that. You hear me, now?"

"I'll tell him. I'll tell him."

"Fine. Now I'm going to let you up. You show as much good sense once you're up as you did just now, you might live a while longer. But don't go doing anything to make me nervous. Shotguns always make me nervous, and this thing's likely to go off if you get jumpy."

He planted a boot in Hobbs' back and put the shotgun against the man's neck again. Then he loosened the rope and worked it up over the man's head. He removed his boot then and backed carefully away, watching Hobbs for any suspicious moves.

As soon as he felt the boot leave, Hobbs craned his neck to see where the shotgun was. When he was sure he was safe, he scrambled to his feet and started backing away toward his horse.

"You remember what I said," Slocum called after him. "You tell your daddy I ain't fixing to bother him. But I aim to get them men I'm after. I don't care what his rules are. And I generally get what I aim for. You tell him that."

"I'll tell him," Hobbs said. "I'll tell him." Then he broke for his horse, swung up into the saddle, and kicked it into a run, heading west along the trail without looking back.

Slocum waited till he was sure the boy was gone. Then he rewound his lariat and mounted up and headed in the other direction.

# 4

Two hours later he was sitting his saddle in the trees above a narrow little clearing, watching a man move manure from a chicken coop to a patch of garden behind a log cabin facing down into the Hole. The clearing stretched up a hillside at the southeast corner of the rim, where the man calling himself Ganning had said he would be. Slocum was in no hurry to ride down and find him. He had no reason to trust Ganning. For all he knew this might be some kind of trap and the man down there a friend of Walker's.

The man wasn't Ganning; he was old enough to be white-haired, though he looked fit enough. He was pushing a homemade wheelbarrow from chicken coop to garden and back again, his breath showing white in the damp, cold day. Down on the left, opposite the chicken coop, was a hound tethered to the front of a small barn, with a muddy lot out back in which Slocum could see one horse. There was no sign of Ganning.

He watched for close to twenty minutes. Then he clucked to the bay and started down out of the trees.

When he got close, the hound went to baying and lunging at the end of its tether. The old man had propped his wheelbarrow against the steps and gone inside the coop, where the chickens raised a sudden clamor; now he came out again, a basket slung from the crook of his elbow, and pitched a stick at the hound.

"Don't keep him tied up, he wears himself out chasing deer. Makes him itchy, though." The old man took a short-stemmed pipe out of his mouth and looked Slocum frankly up and down. "Will's gone off. Be back directly. You'd be John Slocum, I figger. I'm Tom Price. You wait till I'm through here, and I'll fix us some coffee."

Still wary, Slocum scanned the clearing. It bottomed out into the Hole about a hundred yards below the house, behind a screen of trees flanking a creek. Smoke rose from a rock chimney up the south side of the cabin. The thing with Hobbs hadn't worked that heat out entirely; he was still too angry to be civil. "When's this Ganning going to be back?"

"Don't know. Didn't say. You'll have to excuse me. I got to gather up my eggs."

Slocum dismounted and stood in the door while Price moved along a row of chicken roosts, reaching a gentle hand under each hen. Despite the cold, he was wearing only a thick wool shirt under wide suspenders, his pants tucked into knee-high boots. The hens clucked and shifted irritably, blinking in that stupid way chickens had.

"You maybe think raising chickens is a strange business for an old man like me." Price brought out an egg from under the next hen, deposited it in his basket, and moved on to the next. "You'd be surprised the price an egg'll bring in a place like this."

"I didn't come here to talk about eggs. You sure Ganning's coming back this afternoon?"

"He'll be back. Said you was to wait." Price eyed him speculatively. "You can wait, can't you? Will

said you was on the prod. Not a patient man, I gather.
Said you come near starting a war in Bushnell's today.
Over one of Hobbs' sons, I hear."

"I didn't like the way he was acting."

"Still, Walter Hobbs more or less runs this place.
That's why it's named for him. He's no man to be
making an enemy of." Price came out of the coop and
closed the door behind him. "Better come on in the
house. You can wait by the fire."

The cabin was dim and cluttered inside, with only
one window front and back. Slocum wiped his boots
on a scrap of hide laid in front of the door and stood
by the fire while Price deposited his egg basket on a
sideboard and started measuring coffee out of a tin
can into a coffee pot. It wasn't much of a place, just
one large room with wooden beds in two corners and
a table and chairs as crude as those he'd found in the
shack he was holed up in. He didn't like being in
here, unable to see out, and he was getting impatient.

"You got any idea what this Ganning friend of
yours has to tell me?"

"Can't say I do." Price poured the coffee pot full
of water from a bucket and dropped in an eggshell.
"Will don't tell me everything he knows. He's a good
one for keeping his mouth shut. Which is a smart
thing for any man that wants to survive in the Hole."

"You're just full of wise sayings, old man."

"For them that's wise enough to listen." Price carried the coffee pot to the hearth, where he slung it on
a metal hook over the fire. "You're kind of edgy, ain't
you? Will told me about that picture you was showing
around. Didn't sound too smart to me."

"I didn't ask you what you thought about it."

Price wiped his hands on his shirt, watching Slocum

with his steady gaze. "I gather you got cause to be on edge," he said. "I'll take that into account." He went back to the sideboard and started putting his eggs away.

A stamping of feet sounded on the back steps, and the door opened and the man named Ganning came in. He wiped his boots on the hide and hung his hat on a peg near the door. "See you got here," he said, studying Slocum with those cool gray eyes. "Wasn't sure you'd make it alive, from the fuss in Bushnell's. I guess you met Tom here."

"We had a little talk. Maybe you wouldn't mind telling me what this is about. I believe you said you could help me."

"Maybe." Ganning shed his sheepskin and slicker, lifted the lid off the coffee pot, and when he saw it wasn't ready yet, sat at the table and went to pulling off his boots. "Quite a display you put on in Bushnell's. Like Bushnell said, Hobbs has rules here. Keep that up and you'll force him to move against you. Then you won't find your men at all."

"I'll keep it in mind. Now, you got something to tell me, or don't you?"

"Tell you what," Ganning said. "I'm going to take a chance on you." He took something from his shirt pocket and tossed it to Slocum. "The wrong people see that, it could get me killed. I'd appreciate your keeping it to yourself."

Slocum turned it in his palm: a five-pointed star with *Deputy U. S. Marshal* etched across the face of it. He looked up to see Ganning watching him. "How come you'd risk showing me this?"

"You don't know me, but it happens I know you. You ran with a friend of mine sometime back. Jack

Carlton. Helped him out of a scrape or two, I understand. He spoke pretty high of you."

"Blackjack Carlton? I thought he was in California."

Ganning took the badge back from him. "He is. Going on five years now. Settled out there with a girl named Betty and made himself a good life. Couldn't have happened to a better man." He got up from the table and padded in his sock feet to a sideboard, where he rummaged around for a tin cup. "I know you been on the wrong side of the law, but I'll overlook that, on account of Jack and Betty Carlton. I'll help you find your men, but I want you out of the Hole soon as you do. And I want you staying out of trouble otherwise."

The coffee was boiling in the pot. Old Tom Price brought a couple more tin cups over and started pouring. Slocum watched him, thinking how a man never knew when his past was going to catch up to him and either help him or harm him. As it happened, Jack Carlton had been a man worth riding the river for. He was glad to hear Carlton had got what he wanted in California.

He took the steaming cup Price handed him. "I don't suppose you'd tell me what you're doing in the Hole."

"Let's say I'm working on something." Ganning was standing by the fire in his socks now, blowing on his coffee, watching Slocum. "Far as anybody knows, I'm just another drifter on the dodge. I want to ease into this crowd gentle-like. You keep thrashing around like a loose cannon, you're going to foul things up. Now tell me what this is all about. You said they're friends of yours, these men you're hunting?"

"Used to be, till we ended up on different sides of a little dispute back in Texas. Nothing personal. They just hired on to a place called the Lazy J, and I had ties to the other side. A woman. I was working for her father."

"And they killed her."

Slocum shrugged. "I was told it was them. They were seen to ride up and go in the house. Way I pieced it together later, they were all drunked up and looking for me. Had a beef about me being on the wrong side. Only I wasn't home. They walked in on Anne taking a bath, and when I got home I found her lying on the kitchen floor where she had the tub set up. Somebody had put a knife in her belly." He felt heat rising in his brain again, threatening to make him go blind. "It was a kitchen knife in her. A butcher knife. Likely she'd snatched it up to keep 'em off her. One of 'em put it in her belly. I aim to find out which one. I aim to kill 'em all."

Ganning was still watching him, studying him. He nodded now, like maybe he was confirming something he'd suspected. "Let me see that picture again."

Slocum fished the picture out of his pocket and handed it over. Ganning carried it to a window, where he held it up to the light and studied it a while. "I've seen 'em. Been in Bushnell's twice in the last two weeks that I know of." He turned to look at Slocum. "This other one with them, this Frank Walker, he a friend of yours, too?"

"I don't even know him to look at. He was already working for the Lazy J when the others signed on there."

Ganning handed the picture back. "Walker is a nephew to Walter Hobbs. Likely that's how he knew to come here."

Slocum saw old man Price watching him from a stool beside the fire. He looked at the picture, slowly letting that news sink in. It wasn't pleasant news. "Means they're likely at Hobbs' place. Means I got Hobbs against me no matter what I do."

"Not necessarily," Ganning said. "Hobbs ain't the usual run of badman. Got a family. Used to be a big property owner in Tennessee. Lost everything he had in the War and come out here bitter as hell. Now he's got himself established, and he wants to live legal. Got a fine herd, got a prize new bull, got three grown sons to carry on his name. I happen to know he wouldn't take Walker and them friends of yours in. Thinks Walker's a bad influence on his sons."

"Didn't know they was already trying to live up to his own reputation," Price said. "Going on a year now. They ride out, rob a bank or a train somewhere, and run back here to hole up. Likely thought it was a lark, playing badman like the old man. Only last time the oldest got shot up. Laying up there at Hobbs' maybe dying right now. First time Hobbs knew what they were up to." With a rag to protect his hand, Price lifted the coffee pot off the fire and poured himself another cup. "Damned near killed Walter Hobbs. From the look of him, I'd say he's sick. Maybe deathly sick. He's lost control over them boys."

"That's what got me sent here," Ganning said. "They robbed a bank in Cowley County last time. Had to shoot their way out of town. Killed a ten-year-old girl in the street, and that got folks riled enough to bring in the marshal's office. But so far we can't prove nothing. I got sent here to see if I can learn when the boys aim to go out again. And where."

Slocum took a last look at the picture and put it away. "Where do you think Walker and them are?"

"I ain't heard. Ain't accepted well enough yet for that. But there's any number of places to shelter in these hills. I'll help you find them, but like I say, I want you out of here soon as it's over. I don't want you fouling me up. And I suggest you stay away from Bushnell's in the meantime."

Slocum put his coffee cup down. "I don't like people telling me where I can go and where I can't. There's things I need and no place but Bushnell's to buy 'em."

Price stood up and tossed his coffee dregs into the fire. "You look like a smart man, Slocum, but you don't act it. You're acting like a man looking to get killed."

"I've had enough of your advice, old man." Slocum got to his feet and put his hat on. "I come here for one thing. Nothing gets in my way till I've done it. I've said this once today, but I'll tell you, too. I got nothing left but trouble. Any time you want to give me advice, you remember that."

Price shrugged. "That's hate talking. I'll tell you something, son, carrying a load of hate around is bad for any man. Put a fever in your brain, you ain't careful. Ruin your life. Like me, now. I lost a good woman twenty years ago. Died, like yours. No reason in the world for her to die. Made me so mad I vowed I'd never let myself want another. Come out here to these hills and lived on hate for years. Ate it like food. Time I saw what it was doing to me, I was too old to live any way different."

"You ate it," Slocum said. "That's the difference. I aim to make somebody else eat it. You should have killed whoever caused her to die."

The old man smiled. "Couldn't. She died in a windstorm back East. A twister. Come out of the south on a hot afternoon and levelled that house like it was a strawstack. I was in town. Didn't even know it till I come along the road and saw that house gone. God caused it, you see. No way I could kill God."

"Well, God didn't cause my woman to die. I'd like to think Frank Walker did, but maybe it was Bob Foley, or Paul Quinn, or Charley Beaumont."

"God causes everything, son."

"Then he's no friend of mine." Slocum turned to Ganning. "I'm obliged for your help. When can we get started on it?"

"Meet me here at dawn tomorrow. We'll start with these hills down here."

"Fine. You tell your friend here to stick to his chickens. I got enough on my mind as it is."

It was near dark when he approached Bushnell's again. Despite what Ganning had said, he had no intention of steering clear. He came up on it from the rear and circled around to dismount at the hitching rail in front. Carrying the shotgun like a pistol conspicuously in one hand, he went into the saloon.

Bushnell was polishing glasses. His hands started under the bar, but the sight of the Greener brought them up empty. "You got brass, walking in here," he said.

Slocum stopped at the end of the bar. All the tables were empty save the one in the rear. David Hobbs was sitting at that table. David Hobbs and four other men.

One of them unwound a pair of long legs and sauntered the length of the room, his hands just brushing a pair of ebony-handled Colts. He had malicious eyes above a three-day growth of beard, and he looked amused about something. "They tell me you're Slocum," he said. "Davey said you'd be back here. I figured you'd be smarter than that. But, seeing as you're here, Mr. Hobbs wants to see you."

Now Slocum saw the older man sitting alongside David Hobbs. The man was watching him, too far away to see what was in his eyes. This was Walter Hobbs, then, who had named this place. Slocum pointed the Greener like a finger at Bushnell. "Bring me whiskey. About two fingers in a glass." He followed the man with the beard back to the corner table, where Walter Hobbs sat hunched over a glass.

"I'm told you want to talk to me."

Hobbs looked at him—rheumy eyes under eyelids heavy as a lizard's. He was going to fat, though his neck looked unnaturally skinny, with enough leathery flesh drooping under his chin to serve a turkey for wattles. And, from the look of him, Price was right: this was a sick man, maybe deathly sick, and rapidly losing the strength that had once made him what he was.

"I hear you caused a ruckus in here today," he said.

"Your boy here caused a ruckus," Slocum said. "I just put a stop to it."

David Hobbs slumped sullenly beside his father. He glanced at the man with the beard, leaning against the wall with a hand propped on a pistol butt, but he wouldn't look at Slocum.

"That ain't the way I heard it," Hobbs said. "Way I heard it, Davey was minding his own business till you come in here."

"You want it that way, fine. Just say I didn't like his face. I still don't like his face. Maybe you better get him out of here before I change his face around a little."

Hobbs blinked a bit. "Friend, you take a lot of liberties for a stranger. Maybe you didn't hear who I am."

"I heard who you are," Slocum said. "I don't particularly like your face, either. You want to start a war?"

Hobbs leaned back in his chair. "Friend, you're standing in a strange place, facing five men you know nothing about, and you're talking like a mad dog. I think you're a little crazy."

"That's a real possibility," Slocum said. "A real interesting possibility. Push me some more and let's find out." He kept his eyes on Hobbs; the others would do nothing without a signal from Hobbs.

"Friend," Hobbs said, "there's a lot of men on the dodge here, and we can't go to fighting amongst ourselves. I made a rule here long before you showed. The rule says there's no trouble in the Hole. You're threatening to make that rule come undone. You're like a mad dog loose in the calf corral, friend. You ain't careful, you'll bring everybody down on you, and then where'll you be?"

"In hog heaven," Slocum said. "I come here to do some killing. I don't mind doing more."

The man with the beard shifted against the wall, but a glance from Hobbs kept him quiet. "Friend, I'll make allowances for you. You're maybe not in your right mind. I heard you had your woman killed. I can understand how that would affect a man. But you understand one thing. You keep your trouble out of the Hole. You find who you're looking for, you let 'em be till you catch 'em outside the Hole. Otherwise I'll have to come looking for you myself."

"One of 'em I'm looking for's your nephew, Hobbs. Frank Walker."

"I heard you said that. I don't believe Frank would do such a thing. But I ain't responsible for Frank. You leave things be in the Hole. You catch Frank outside it, that's his lookout." Hobbs pushed his chair back and got to his feet. "Now I'm going to trust you'll heed what I say. If you don't, I'll hear about it. Then every man's hand will be against you." He touched a hand to his hat. "Good day, friend. Davey, you come on."

David Hobbs started to protest, but a look from his father shut him up. He sidled sullenly past Slocum and joined the others headed toward the door. Slocum watched them go, aware of Bushnell eyeing him from the bar. Walter Hobbs might have been a man to reckon with once, but it was clear he wanted to avoid trouble now if he could. If things felt right, maybe he would stay out of this till it was over.

Slocum turned and headed past Bushnell into the store. He needed some lard for his skillet and some candles to light the shack and maybe a sack of beans. And, just to be on the safe side, a lot more shells for the Greener.

# 5

He came up the hill south of the shack just after nightfall. He was looking forward to shelter after a long wet day, but forty yards down the slope he sent the bay abruptly off the trail and drew rein in the trees.

A glow of firelight showed through the deerhide he had stretched over the windows. What fire he had left in the hearth should be out by now. Somebody was in there.

Likely it was somebody on the dodge, but he had staked his claim clear enough: He'd left his gear in there, and his packhorse was still picketed in the orchard. Anybody brazen enough to move into a place already occupied would surely be ready to fight for it. He dismounted, retrieved the Greener from where it was lashed under his slicker back of the saddle, and started up through the trees toward the shack.

He made a slow, careful circle of the place and found no horses but his own. Whoever was in there had arrived afoot. He shoved two fresh shells into the Greener, in case the others had got wet, and crept up to lean his ear against the rear door.

There was no sound from inside. Carefully, he took hold of the knob and turned it till he heard the latch click. Then he kicked the door open and threw himself back against the wall.

The sudden move put him in a blur. It was a moment before his head cleared, before he realized he'd heard somebody cry out inside. The sound of it was still dying away in his ear.

The voice of a woman.

The door had swung back partly closed. He reached out to push it open again. When that brought no response, he stepped halfway in through the door, the shotgun levelled at the room.

The woman was at the table, staring wide-eyed at him, both hands clutched over her mouth. One look showed him the room was empty except for her, lit only by the fire and the one candle she'd stuck on the table-top. He took a quick scan of what little he could see outside.

"You alone?"

She nodded and brought her hands down, and now he saw it was the waitress from Bushnell's, the girl called Susan. She couldn't have been here long. She was still bundled up like a rag doll in a bulky man's coat, wearing mittens and a shawl, and everything she had on was dripping wet.

He lowered the shotgun. "I thought Bushnell's put you up."

"Mrs. Bushnell threw me out." She looked dead tired, too tired to hide the shame on her face. "She didn't mind men like that Hobbs trying what he tried. Bushnell was a different thing. He's been trying since I been there. Today she caught him at it."

He could see the effort it cost her to meet his eyes. Some hungry little spasm wriggled alive in his belly, triggered by the sight of that lush ripe mouth, by the pain and the need in those big eyes. Even bundled up as she was he could see her breasts swelling out that bulky coat. The memory of Anne alive and naked in his arms passed quickly through his mind, faded to become the sight of her dead on the floor in that house in Johnson County. He felt a flicker of revulsion pass across his face, saw the girl wince and look away, and tried to get himself under control. He'd been alone with this anger so long he'd forgotten how it must appear to other people.

"I was going to walk to Coffey," she said, like maybe she owed him an explanation. "Ninety miles. Then I remembered this place. I stayed here for a week last spring. It was empty then."

"You can't stay here now. I got things to do. You'd be in the way." He saw a bedroll now, on the floor beside her chair, and a large bundle wrapped in a blanket and tied with rope. "Surely there's someplace else you can go."

"Mrs. Bushnell said I should try Hobbs' place. Said that David fellow would take me." Defiance showed in the set of her mouth. "I'd rather walk to Coffey."

"Ain't there some way you can get to Coffey without walking?"

She thought about that. "Bushnell sends a wagon out once a month for supplies. Usually Joe takes it. Joe's the cook." She was studying his face now, as if trying to read his mind. "I know you're after somebody, but I could be a help to you. I could cook. I could clean. I wouldn't get in your way."

"I don't need any help. When's the next wagon out?"

"The last day of the month." She was still studying his face, watching his eyes. "Joe's been a friend to me. He'd take me with him. I could be waiting for him down on the road if you'd let me stay till then."

He figured this had to be an ordeal for her, getting thrown out of bed and board, afoot and friendless

ninety miles from nowhere. It was three weeks till the
end of the month. The idea of sharing this small shack
with a woman made him uneasy, especially a woman
as lush as this one was, but he couldn't put her out.

"You can stay here till the wagon leaves," he said.
"Not a day longer." Then he went out and closed the
door on her so he wouldn't have to listen to her thanks.

It took him half an hour to see to his horses and
make sure they were secure for the night. When he'd
stowed his saddle in the woodshed, he rapped once
on the door to give her warning and went back inside,
carrying the rifle scabbard and the shotgun, the slicker
draped over his shoulder. The girl had her outer gar-
ments off and was standing before the fire, peeling
her dress down to her waist. That spasm wriggled
alive in his belly again till he saw she had another
dress on under the first, wearing two to give her less
to carry.

She flushed and turned her back, wriggling the
outer dress down over her hips. He pulled his eyes
away and stowed his rifle and shotgun in the corner.

"There's some beans left in that pot," he said, and
returned the photograph to its place in the mirror on
the wall. "I killed some squirrels and hung them out
in that shed yesterday. I'll bring one in and we can
cook up some supper."

She helped him cook the squirrel, but there was an
awkward silence between them all through supper. He
couldn't help looking at her body, and he didn't know
where to put his eyes. The nearness of her was tightening his throat and making him angry at the same
time. She wouldn't look at him, and that gave him an
idea how hard this was for her, too, knowing nothing
about him except what she'd seen in Bushnell's: part

good, part bad—a man who'd stood up for her but who looked to be as dangerous as the men he was hunting, the men he'd called his friends.

Friends. He wasn't exactly young anymore, and by now he knew a man didn't meet up with too many others he could talk to in a lifetime. And these had been the best in a long while, the old ease always there even when they met up again after years of being apart. Looking at them in that picture on the wall made him feel the same way he felt looking at the girl—anger seething there where he didn't expect anger to be, hate all tangled up with good feelings and good memories. It made him want to slash the air around him, cut away the trash, so he could see things straight again.

The rain had started again. The scraping of the girl's spoon was a tiny sound under the drumming of the roof. She had her eyes down, like a proper schoolgirl uncertain of her welcome. He took advantage of it to look at her: the long dark lashes, the oval face, the lush mouth, those astonishing breasts straining the bodice of her dress.

"How'd you come to stay in this place last spring?"

She threw him a glance and flushed and looked down at her plate again. "The man I was with found it. We'd just got here. I only stayed a week." She nodded toward the mirror and caught his eye again. "You always stare at that picture like that?"

He shrugged. "I suppose I do. It's all I've had for company for months."

"That's the picture you had in Bushnell's today. The men you're looking for." Shyly, she studied his face. "You really aim to go against them? All alone the way you are?"

"I didn't ride all the way from Texas for nothing else."

Her fork picked at the meat on her plate. "That's what Jesse was after. The man I came here with. Chasing a man that done him out of some money. I couldn't get him not to come, so I came with him. We fought about it right here in this room. Then one day I was in Bushnell's buying some eggs and Mrs. Bushnell offered me a job. I thought maybe he'd see I meant business then—Jesse, I mean—so I took it."

"And did he? See you meant business?"

"I never had a chance to find out. That was the day he caught up with the man he was chasing. The other man killed him. I been staying at Bushnell's ever since."

She was watching her fork push a piece of meat around on her plate, looking more resigned than sad. After a bit she glanced back up at him. "Are you always so . . . so suspicious?"

"What do you mean?"

"The way you came in the door. With the shotgun."

"A man gets used to living that way. You cross trails with a lot of men in this country. Some of them take a dislike to you. There's men would kill me if they could. Not just the ones I'm hunting."

"Seems a poor way to live."

He watched her eyes watching his, wondering if he agreed with her. It seemed he'd always lived like that, ever since the War, since he was a boy almost. He never went anywhere without some part of his mind directed toward his back, some part of him listening for a warning sound, some part of him watching for a man looking to do him harm. Sometimes he could let his guard down. He remembered holing up in Mexico once with a shapely brown girl who spoke no English and liked to raise hell all night same as he did and who always took him home to her bed at dawn and woke him with hot black coffee the next afternoon. That had been a good time. But even then he got restless after a while. He could relax only so long. Then something got to pushing at him from inside till he had to find some way to get the old feeling back— that keen awareness that came from knowing you were walking with danger. Without danger he didn't feel alive anymore.

He tried to change only once, with Anne. He had let his guard down then, like every woman wanted a man to do, and it had been his undoing. He wouldn't do it again.

"I want to thank you for what you told David Hobbs in Bushnell's today," she said. "Not many men would say a thing like that."

Those big soft eyes flicked at him again, full of something he couldn't quite read, and he had to pull his eyes away to keep from staring at the way the cloth tightened across her breasts when she breathed. The nearness of her, defenseless and needy and voluptuous as she was, was getting to be more than he could stand. He pushed his chair back from the table.

"There's a bucket out in that shed. I'll bring some rainwater in and you can dump them dishes in it if you want. Then we better bed down."

# 6

While she did the dishes he dug a bottle and a stolen glass out of his pack and sat at the table and brooded on that picture on the wall. When she'd finished he drove a horseshoe nail into the chimney with the butt of his Colt and hung a blanket on a rope strung from a nail to the opposite wall, and she took her bedroll and bundle back into the corner behind the blanket, where she could have some privacy. Uncomfortably aware of her moving around back there, he laid his own bedroll up close to the fire, stripped to the skin the way he always slept, and climbed into his blankets.

He found she wasn't shielded as much as she thought she was. She'd taken the candle back in there with her, and now the light was throwing her shadow on the wall clear as anything he'd seen in a lantern show. He tried to put his mind on tomorrow—the chance of Ganning helping him find the men in that picture on the wall—but the sounds of her moving around wouldn't let him think, and he lay helpless in his bedroll watching that shapely shadow shedding clothes on the corner wall. He watched the hair come undone, watched her shake it down below her shoulders, watched the shadow squirm and wriggle some last flimsy undergarment down her legs. He could tell she was naked now, her heavy breasts jostling and jiggling even in shadow as she bent to lift what was likely a nightgown from a pile of clothes and pull it down over her head. Then the shadow moved, and she came out from behind the blanket, knelt in front of the fire, and began combing out her hair.

Heat flared up in him. She was in profile to him, her back arched, both hands up working at her hair, and that nightgown was so thin he could see through it like it wasn't even there. He had to work some just to find breath enough to speak.

"I see why Bushnell's woman got you fired. You show yourself like that to Bushnell every night?"

Both hands came down out of her hair and clutched the comb in her lap, but she wouldn't look at him. Something close to resentment had come into the set of her face. "I could have done that," she said. "Maybe pretty soon I would have." She took a quick look at his face and glanced away. "You got any idea what it's like being a woman in a place like this? Knowing you can't survive without a man, and not much in the way of men to pick from? I've never done what you're thinking, though. I've always tried to make it on my own. And look where it's got me."

"So you figure to try it the other way now. I look like a better meal ticket than the others?"

Her eyes came up to meet his, and this time she didn't look away. "I said I'd be on the next wagon out. I meant what I said. I still mean it."

"Then how come you're sitting there half-naked?"

"We're stuck here together. You'll get around to it sooner or later. Might as well make it sooner."

"Somebody ought to learn you some manners." He fumbled for the stub of a cheroot in the clothes he'd laid alongside his bedroll, so angry his hands trembled when he struck a match. "You think I'm too much of an animal to control myself? I never want a woman in my bed unless she wants to be there."

She went back to staring at the comb in her lap, a slow flush creeping up her face. "I didn't say I didn't want to be in your bed."

He recognized the signs. He knew what she was after, despite what she'd said and the resigned way she'd said it. It was a game certain women played, and the rules were as fixed as the rules for five-card stud. Stick around any saloon woman long enough and you'd find her playing it. She wanted in your bed, and she wanted nothing else, and when the time came to move on she wouldn't make a fuss. Sometimes she even convinced herself it was true. But stay around long enough and it always turned out she wanted more. He could see it coming every time; the trouble was, he couldn't resist the bait when it was offered.

But something in him was too angry to take it the way he usually did. Something in him wanted to make her work for it. "Let me hear you say it." He sucked on the cheroot, watching her try to avoid his eyes, surprised himself at how cold his voice sounded. "Let me hear you say you want in my bed."

She was still clutching that comb in her lap, and she still wouldn't meet his eyes. He could tell by the rise and fall of her breasts that she was having trouble getting enough breath, and now he saw her nipples start to harden and come erect.

She tried to speak, swallowed once, and tried again. When she finally got it out, it was little more than a murmur. "I want to be in your bed."

He took a last drag on the cheroot and flung it into the fire. "Come here."

Still clutching that comb in her lap like a shield,

eyes downcast, she rose into a half-crouch and crept across to kneel beside his bedroll. He had to swallow hard himself, watching those big breasts wobble and quiver as she moved, seeing the openness in those big eyes she lifted now to meet his own. Then that heat rose up unbearable in him, and he seized her night-gown at the throat and tore it hem to hem.

She flinched, stripped suddenly naked in the fire-light, breasts quivering heavily, one shredded sleeve slipping down her arm. Then he kicked the blankets off grabbed her by the wrist, and pulled her to him.

He took her with something like distaste, his cal-loused hands rough on the softness of her flesh, mov-ing with the heat of urgency, hating her even as he took his pleasure of her, even as he heard her gasp and cry out in response, even as he felt that astonishing body arch and writhe against his, her eyes closed, her hands clutching at his shoulders, her stifled murmurs growing gradually into hot and helpless cries.

He recoiled from her as soon as it was over. He pulled away and lay alongside her, but even that was too close, and he rose and cleaned himself on what remained of her nightgown and moved to pour a glass of whiskey at the table. He still couldn't seem to get enough breath.

She stayed sprawled on her back in front of the fire, making no attempt to shield herself from his eyes. He drank the whiskey off neat, feeling it burn down inside him, clearing its own hot path through the heat of what had just happened between them. She was such a shapely sight he could barely stand to look at her.

The heat was still beating through him, and the words came crowding up his throat before he could curb them. "I just tied myself to one woman. I don't want to tie myself to another. You just remember one thing. No matter what happens, I want you on that next wagon out."

Without taking his eyes off her, he fished up his makings and set about rolling himself a smoke, surprised to find his hands shaking as he crimped the paper and shook a line of tobacco down the crease. He poured another drink, set a match to the cigarette, and stood there breathing hard, his hands shaking, watching her watching him.

# 7

For a week he scoured the hills with Ganning.

Unable to sleep, he left the shack every morning before dawn, often catching Price and Ganning before either had had breakfast, too impatient himself to accept more than coffee before urging Ganning out and into the saddle. They squared off sections of the rim around the Hole, taking a section a day, quitting each section only when they were sure it was clear. By the fourth day they had checked out three shacks, one of them empty, the others occupied by men Ganning recognized, and Slocum's restlessness was growing. He would begin each day more impatient than the last, combing the country for sight of Beaumont or Foley or Quinn, hunting them like a thirsty man looking for water, too driven to slow down. Often after leaving Ganning at the end of the day he would continue on alone, searching some likely place for a camp—a gully, or a cave, or a clearing he'd sighted through the trees—only giving up when the approach of night drove him back to the shack and the girl.

That edginess was still there between them. He could tell she was waiting for him to loosen up, but it was all he could do to remain civil and stay out of her way. She did all the cooking now, helped chop and carry firewood, and toward the end of the week she even heated water in an iron pot she'd found in

53

the woodshed and washed both her clothes and his and hung them on the rope that stretched across the room between them. He didn't like her taking that wifely role for granted, but talking to her about it was more conversation than he wanted, so he just let her do as she liked.

She had a cooked meal waiting for him every night when he got back, but it was more than just her acting like a wife that made him wary. Looking at her never failed to bring blood surging into his brain. The sight of that lush mouth and the large dark eyes, her body was so astonishing that he could feel his palms itch from wanting to lay hands on her. He would have to take his eyes off her then, but even so he could tell the look on his face scared her a bit. As if sensing his mood, she would remain silent all through supper, and afterward, while she washed up, he would bring out the bottle and glass and begin that nightly drinking he'd needed now for months to get him anywhere near sleep.

She had taken to joining him at the table after supper, pouring some whiskey in a cracked china cup and sipping at it like maybe she needed company. He figured she wanted to talk, but he was intent on his own thoughts, brooding at that picture stuck into the mirror on the wall, and just sensing her at his elbow was enough to put him on edge. Once, maybe made bold by whiskey, she tried to break through his silence. They'd been sitting there for two hours, and he was aware she'd been trying to catch his eye for a long time, but he didn't want to look at her.

"You hadn't ought to sit here like this," she said finally, shy and hesitant, like maybe she was afraid what his response might be. "Anybody can see staring at that picture's bad for you. You ought to see your face."

"I've seen my face," he said. "I see it every morning when I shave. And what I do with that picture's my business."

She fell silent, looking at her glass. After a while, she tried again. "You're just like Jesse was."

"Your friend from last spring?" He looked at her then, meeting those large pained eyes, blatantly and without disguise staring at those astonishing breasts, watching her flinch when she saw where he was looking. "No, I ain't like him. He was too dumb to live. He went and got himself killed to prove it."

She didn't look away, though he continued to stare directly at her breasts, though the angry heat of his desire was so strong he could practically smell it in the room.

"It's like a cancer in you," she said. "A person can see it eating you up. You don't sleep more than four hours a night. You don't eat. You're out in that cold every day. And then you come back in the evening and sit there and drink and stare at that picture. It's going to kill you, you ain't careful."

He went back to brooding at the picture, and after a while she retreated behind her blanket. But after he'd crawled into his bedroll that night she came out naked save for a short little shift incapable of containing that astonishing body and crept in with him under his blankets. Three times that week she made the short trip from her corner to his bedroll, always with that sad and needful look on her face, always naked save for that tiny shift that her breasts caused to wobble and move like cannonballs loose under a blanket, and she was always already moist between her thighs, the small sounds already starting in her throat as he entered her.

They never talked then. He took her wordlessly and without love each time, working himself into a state of blind oblivion, trying to rid himself of that obsession she didn't like to see and he didn't want to feel. And he recoiled from her every time afterward, lay cold and angry beside her, not wanting to see what was on her face, not wanting to see that voluptuous body sprawled out naked and inviting in the reddish glow of the fire. Sometimes she fell asleep at his side, but always when he woke she was gone, back to her own bedroll behind that blanket, as if she didn't want to wake beside him any more than he wanted to wake beside her. So he was glad to rise every morning before dawn, glad to saddle up and be gone into the drizzling rain, searching the hills with Ganning for that bunch from Jackson County.

It was on Friday of that week, scouting the south rim of the Hole, that he found the first sign of them. It was just past noon. He was leading the way down a narrow hogback when he caught the smell of horses somewhere below him. He dismounted and led the bay down through trees still dripping rainwater till he saw what it was: a one-room shanty with a small corral out back, maybe fifty yards below him. He was already working the focus on his field glasses when he heard Ganning hunker down in the brush beside him.

The place was occupied. There were horses in the corral, and smoke rose from the rock chimney running up the near wall. The cabin faced half-right, down a narrow clearing; he could see the rear door beyond the corral but no windows.

He lowered the glasses and handed them to Ganning. "Take a look."

Ganning worked the focus, scanning the ground around the cabin. "You think it's them?"

"Got to be. That paint in the corral's Charley Beaumont's horse. You see anybody?"

"Not a soul. They're likely inside out of the wet."

Slocum took the glasses back and focussed on the corral again. He counted nine horses besides the paint. Only two saddles, one a packsaddle from the shape of it, under a tarp on the top rail, but likely they'd taken the rest in out of the rain.

"Ten horses," he said. "A packhorse apiece would make eight. Either they got a couple of spares or there's another man or two in there with them."

"Or they're not using packhorses and there's a good half-dozen in there with them. What you aim to do now?"

Slocum rose from his crouch to stuff the field glasses back in his saddlebags. "I aim to flush 'em out and kill 'em."

Ganning looked at him. "I knew you were reckless. I didn't know you were crazy. You can't do it. At best, you got four men against you. More likely nine or ten. The two off us couldn't do it, assuming I'd be crazy enough to go along with you."

"We can do it." Slocum retrieved his shotgun from where it was lashed on back of the saddle. "You cover the front. I'll climb that tree by the corner, drop a saddle blanket over the chimney, and cover the back. The smoke'll drive 'em out."

Ganning shook his head. "You may be crazy. I didn't say I was."

"Fine." Slocum shed his slicker and hung it on his saddlehorn. "You go on. I get on the other side of that cabin, I ought to be able to cover both doors."

He stuffed both sheepskin pockets with cartridges

for the shotgun and his Winchester, then crouched in the dripping brush again and broke the Greener open. He shoved two shells into the breech, clicked the shotgun closed, and hung it by its sling from one shoulder. Then he drew his Colt and checked the loads in the chamber. He was just sliding his Winchester out of its saddle boot when Ganning sighed and got to his feet.

"All right," Ganning said. "Go ahead. Get up that tree. I'll cover the front." He drew his own Winchester then and started down through the brush.

Slocum hunkered in the brush, watching Ganning, thinking of those men in the cabin. Somewhere inside him was a hunk of memory he had walled himself off from, and he could feel it trying to work itself free. Memories of every man in there save Walker, memories of good times and bad, going back a good number of years. He wouldn't let himself think on that. Instead he concentrated on Ganning.

Ganning had worked his way down through the brush till he was as close to the far end of the cabin as he could get without leaving cover. He was edged up against a tree trunk down there now, just opposite the front corner. Slocum could see him judging the distance, watching the ground in front. After the space of a long breath, he set himself and dashed for the corner of the cabin.

He fetched up against the wall and flattened himself against it, waiting, his eyes on Slocum. Slocum raised his hands, palms up, to say he'd seen no reaction.

Ganning waited a moment more. Then he eased his head around the corner. When he'd scanned the ground in front of the cabin, he ran for the creek, angling down past the other side.

Slocum waited five minutes after Ganning had disappeared into the brush along the creekbank. When
he was sure nobody had seen, he returned his Winchester to its saddle boot. Too awkward, carring both
rifle and shotgun, and he wouldn't need the rifle with
Ganning helping. Then, moving in a bent-over crouch,
he started down through the brush toward the corral.

He found what he was looking for under the tarpaulin—a saddle blanket draped over the packsaddle
on the top rail, just where he'd expected it to be.
Quickly, he dipped the blanket in the rain barrel standing under the eaves and draped it wet and dripping
over his shoulder. Then he climbed the corral rails till
he could reach the nearest limb and swung himself
up into the tree.

The tree stood maybe ten yards from the chimney.
Smoke was coiling up at a pretty good lick, rising to
lie flat as a fogbank in the wet and heavy air. Slocum
worked his way up till he was a yard or two above
the chimney, the shotgun swinging from its sling, the
saddle blanket dripping on his legs. When he was high
enough, he eased down flat on a tree limb angling
toward the chimney and started snaking his way out
along its length.

The limb was leafless and slick with rain and not
much bigger around than his arm. Slowly, he inched
out toward the tip. Twice he had to stop and resettle
the shotgun sling to keep the Greener from sliding
down his arm, and once he almost lost the blanket.
He was maybe halfway there when he felt the limb
begin to give beneath him.

He stopped, holding his breath. The limb sagged,
groaned, cracked a little, and then held. Even so, it
was so narrow here he could barely hold on, and

slanting down so steep he was close to falling off on his face. He worked the blanket off his shoulder with one hand, lowered it to arm's length, and began swinging it carefully back and forth. When he had enough momentum worked up, he let fly toward the chimney.

He almost overshot the target. The blanket hit square, but the near side flapped up and almost over. Only the weight of a water-soaked corner brought it back down to close off the chimney mouth. Slocum watched till he was sure the smoke was choked off, then shinnied back down off the tree.

Quickly, watching the back door, moving again in that bent-over crouch, the shotgun up and ready now, he skirted around the corral, heading toward the creek. He paused at the corner of the cabin only long enough to see that the one window on the far side had deerhide stretched across it. Then he ran for the shelter of a tree in the brush along the creek. He wanted to be in place before the smoke flushed out whoever was in there.

He crouched down behind the tree trunk and drew his Colt, getting his breath back. Too far away to do much harm now with the Greener. Forty yards down the creekbank, he saw Ganning hunkered behind a similar tree. He caught Ganning's eye, but Ganning shook his head. He settled on his haunches and waited.

He couldn't see the front, but he had the back door still in sight, that and the hided-over window. After a while, smoke began seeping through the crack at the top of the door. Just an occasional wisp at first, then a steady stream coming from several places.

He waited, watching, but there was no sound from inside. Then smoke began drifting up below the eaves,

as if filtering out from under the roof. Still no sign
of life. Whoever was in there must be asleep. The
whole place was leaking smoke, like a pot steaming
on a stove.

Then he heard somebody coughing inside, a loud,
choking cough that sounded like somebody strangling.
He brought his Colt up and held steady on the door.

A long moment passed. He didn't hear the cough
again. He was beginning to think maybe the smoke
had beat him to it when something hit the hide over
the window.

He caught only the sound the first time. The second
time he was watching the window and saw the sudden
bulge in the hide when something hit it from the other
side. Then again, and again, and again. Somebody
was trying to bash that deerhide away from the window.

He swung the Colt to cover the window. One corner
of the hide came loose, and smoke boiled out and
settled into a constant upward stream. Now Slocum
saw the steady swing of a rifle butt striking what
remained of the hide—somebody pretty frantic from
the look of it. Whoever it was was standing just out
of sight, but a savvy man could judge where. And a
man in a hurry could kill the other where he stood—
put a bullet right through that thin wall. Slocum wasn't
in a hurry. He wanted some answers first.

The deerhide was hanging by one corner now. The
bashing had ceased. Smoke was pouring out. It was
too dark inside to see anything, and all sounds had
stopped.

Slocum put the Colt back to covering the door.
"Charley? Bob? You in there? This is Slocum."

A sudden *whomp* at the back door sent him diving

for the ground. When he realized what it was, he raised up to peer over the brush.

The door was still swinging back and forth on its hinges, but it was open now. Smoke spilled out the top like some kind of topsy-turvy waterfall. Something hit the door from the other side again, and he saw it was a stick of firewood, jammed in place to hold the door open. He got a glimpse of one hand and an arm, and then hand and arm both were snatched out of sight.

"Charley? Charley, I want to talk to you."

Still no response. They had to know his voice, even if they hadn't caught the name. From inside the cabin he heard a rush of steam as somebody doused the fire in the fireplace. From the look of things, they weren't aiming to let that smoke flush them out of there.

Now the same *whomp* of sound came from the front end, and he saw smoke pouring up from where the front door had slammed open. Ganning had his Winchester covering it, but he wasn't moving. Nobody was showing himself down there, either.

"Charley, you in there?"

From somewhere inside the cabin came a voice he didn't recognize: "Ain't nobody named Charley in here."

He looked at Ganning, but Ganning just shrugged. It could be Frank Walker. He wouldn't recognize Walker's voice. Or it could be the extra horses belonged to men in there he didn't know. If he could get them separated, get the strangers out, things would be a lot easier.

"I want Charley Beaumont," he called. "Beaumont, Foley, Walker and Quinn. Anybody else I got no quarrel with."

Something fell or was knocked over inside the cabin, a table or a chair. "Ain't no Charley Beaumont in here. Nor any of them others. Whoever you are, mister, you got the wrong place."

"You tell me why Charley Beaumont's horse is in that corral, then."

A long silence set in. Then: "That feller. He left here this morning. Him and his friends." Another silence. Then, like an afterthought: "That horse is lame."

Slocum took a harder look at the corral. The paint stood against the near rail, head down, like maybe it was half asleep. Its weight was all on three legs, the right front hoof cocked up and resting weightless on the ground, but that didn't mean anything. That was just the way a horse liked to stand sometimes. He dug around at his feet till he found a good-sized pebble and pitched it toward the corral.

The pebble struck the paint in the haunch. The hide rippled along its back, but it didn't move.

Slocum dug around in the earth till he found a rock nearly as big as his fist and heaved that one after the first. The rock struck the ground just outside the corral, bounced once, and hit the paint on one rear fetlock. The paint jerked its head up and limped away across the corral, favoring that right front hoof.

It was lame, all right. Which proved absolutely nothing. That still could be Walker talking in there. Or somebody sharing a cabin out of the rain with men he didn't know.

"You in there. Come on out and get clear. I got nothing against you. I want them that's in there with you."

"I believe you," the man called back, "like I believe the rain ain't wet. Ain't nobody in here with me. Them fellers left here this morning. They was already packed and moving when I got here."

Ganning rose to his feet and started working his way farther down through the brush along the creek-bank, watching the cabin. Slocum figured he was trying to get a line of sight through the front door. He went maybe ten yards and stopped to rest his Winchester in the crook of a low-lying limb, still covering the front.

"You can't get out of there," Ganning called. "We got the window and both doors covered. Suppose you come out where we can see you. If what you say is true, you got nothing to worry about."

Another long silence set in. Whoever was doing the talking had to be unhappy to learn there was more than one man against him. Slocum could hear the sounds of somebody moving around in the cabin. Likely they were getting set for a siege.

He started working his way down through the brush toward Ganning, keeping his eye on the window. The smoke had thinned considerably. He got a look in through the window now, but from low along the creekbank all he could see was a bit of the rafters and the rock of the chimney climbing the far wall. He crept down along the creek to where Ganning was and sheltered in behind a nearby tree.

"You seen anybody in there?"

"Can't," Ganning said. "Door opens the wrong way."

"What about the voice? Sound like Walker?"

"Never talked to him long enough to say. You sure it's them in there? Maybe this man's telling the truth."

"Don't know. Could be they're playing possum, thinking I'll buy his story and move on. You keep him talking. I want to get close enough to see in."

"Watch yourself. He might be setting you up."

"I'll chance it. You keep him busy."

He left the shelter of his tree and moved back up the brushrow to the position he had left. Nothing had changed that he could see. The stick of firewood still held the door propped open. The paint stood against the far rail of the corral now, head down, right hoof cocked up and resting weightless on the ground. What smoke was left was drifting lazily out of the cracks around the eaves.

Ganning called out from down the creekbank: "You're going to have to come out of there sooner or later. Better make it now, before things get worse."

"Why'n't you just go on off and leave me alone?" the man answered. "Them fellers you're looking for done left. You can see their tracks out there."

"What's to prove you're alone in there?"

"Who said I was? I just said your men ain't here."

Slocum was filling his pockets with pebbles from the creekbank, trying to judge by the man's voice where he was in there. The man was awfully quick to deny he was alone. Which maybe meant he *was* alone and less able to defend himself than he wanted known. Could be he had stolen the horses and had the law or somebody after him.

His pockets filled, Slocum studied what he could see of the cabin. He knew where he would be if it was him in there: with that rock fireplace behind him, and snug up against it, where it would protect his back. And if that was where this man was, he himself ought to be able to work his way around to that door without being seen. He started up through the brush toward the crest of the hogback the cabin was sitting on.

It took him only five minutes. By then he had

circled around and came down along the near side of
the corral. The man was telling the truth about one
thing, anyway: four sets of tracks led up away from
the corral, crossing the spine of the ridge and disappearing down through the timber on the other side.
Judging by the prints, one of them was a mule. And
they were fresh. They could have been laid that morning. He would find out soon enough.

With the cabin between them now, he could barely
hear Ganning trying to talk the man outside. He went
along the corral, lowering rails to the ground. The
horses milled around some inside, but they made no
move toward the opening. Time enough for that. He
holstered the Colt and unslung the shotgun from his
shoulder. Then he crept over beside the door.

The man inside was repeating himself to Ganning:
"Them fellers you're looking for rode out not more'n
an hour ago. Four of them. One of them wearing a
beard, one of them a Mex. Or half Mex." Again there
was a silence, and again the man added what seemed
an afterthought: "That paint belonged to the bearded
feller. He's the one riding the mule."

Slocum could see in now, along the wall with the
window in it, almost to the far door. He couldn't see
anything but the wall, but he marked where the voice
was coming from—back near the fireplace, like he'd
figured. Holding the Greener in his left hand, he
brought out a handful of pebbles from his sheepskin
pocket.

Ganning's voice came from beyond the cabin:
"Where'd they say they were headed?"

"Mister, you can make me eat smoke, but you can't
make me do your dirty work. Follow them tracks,
and find out for yourself."

Slocum braced himself and flung the pebbles in toward the far corner.

He shouted, "Freeze!" when the clatter came and ducked in the door.

Pebbles ricocheted around the walls. He had both barrels of the Greener cocked, leveled at the table upturned before the hearth. The man behind it was holding a big Sharps rifle on the far door, but the shout had yanked his head around toward Slocum. He was the only man in the cabin.

"Easy," Slocum said. "I got double-ought buck in this thing. You told it straight—you got nothing to worry about." Out the window, he saw Ganning holding his Winchester on the far door. "Ganning? They cleared out, like he said. Get them horses down here."

He saw now that this was hardly more than a boy, short and slight, with a bushy black beard and bushy black hair to match. And he looked to be wondering if he could get that rifle around in time.

"Don't try it," Slocum said. "We ain't after you. Just dump that rifle."

The boy was staring at Slocum with bulging black eyes, and now Slocum saw the bulging wasn't caused by fright, it was natural to him, some affliction that made him look continually surprised, like maybe he beheld visions other people couldn't see. He hesitated, then dumped the Sharps on the floor in front of the table.

"Now put your hands in the air and kind of push that table away with your feet," Slocum said.

The boy did as he was told—hunkered down on the floor and pushed the table away with both feet. He had a gunbelt laid out on the floor beside him, a box of .50 caliber shells for the Sharps beside that,

and a Navy Colt on the floor on either side of him.
Ready for a siege, even outnumbered as he was. For
sure he'd stolen the horses in the corral.

"Slide those guns over here," Slocum said. "We'll
be wanting to get away from here without worrying
about our backs. You'll be all right. I'll leave 'em
outside."

The boy looked at him with those bug eyes. Despite
his youth, the beard made him look preternaturally
old, like one of those taciturn hill people Slocum
remembered from the Georgia of his youth. "Why
should I trust you?" he said. "What's to keep you
from killing me once you got my guns?"

Slocum waggled the shotgun at him. "What's to
keep me from killing you right now? Come on. Kick
'em over here."

Outside, he heard Ganning leading the horses down
through the brush to the corral. He was impatient now,
thinking of how close he'd come, how close those
four men were, riding not more than an hour away
somewhere south of this ridge, at the other end of
those tracks outside.

"Come on, move, before I lose my patience."

Keeping his hands up in the air, the boy propped
a boot behind each of the weapons and kicked them
spinning across the floor to Slocum's feet. Holding
the Greener on him with one hand, Slocum picked
each one of them up and pitched it out the door behind
him. He could see Ganning already in the saddle out
there, holding the bay by the reins at the corner of
the corral.

He gave the boy a last look at the muzzles of the
Greener. "Just stay put till we're gone. Then you can
get your guns back."

He ducked back out the door then and ran for the corral. Inside it, he snatched the tarpaulin off the packsaddle and ran at the horses, whooping and flapping the air with the tarp. The horses spooked and went careening around the corral, spilling out the opening where he'd let the rails down. He chased them across the yard toward the creek and watched them fan out at a run down the clearing north of the cabin, the paint hobbling only a couple dozen yards before limping to a halt. Then he dropped the tarp and ran for the bay.

The bay was dancing, wanting to join that stampede down the clearing. Ganning grabbed it by the bridle while Slocum stuck a boot in the stirrup and swung up into the saddle. He trotted the bay out to where he could see those horses heading away through the tall grass.

"That ought to hold him for a while," he said. "Let's get after them. They got at least an hour's start."

He reined the bay around, kicked it up over the spine of the ridge, and started down the other side.

# 8

They followed the trail south down through the timber. Slocum stayed in the lead, head down, watching the tracks. He could feel that fire burning in him again, eagerness whipping him on, and he kept the bay trotting even down the steep, brushy slope. He sensed Ganning was letting him have his head, keeping the roan just back of the bay's hindquarters, not saying anything. He knew Ganning thought he was a little crazed, and maybe he was, but that was his business. He would be rid of it as soon as this was over. An hour's start could be made up. He could catch them before the day was gone.

He came down out of the brush at the bottom of the slope and reined up so fast the bay skidded in the mud. A narrow trail branched east and west along a shallow little creek here, the creek running so fast it was showing white water. The tracks separated now, the three horses turning west up the trail, the mule splitting off and heading on east alone. Slocum was down out of the saddle examining the tracks when Ganning pulled up beside him.

"One of them's heading out," Ganning said. "This trail swings around back of Price's. Connects up with the road just east of your place. Whoever's on the mule's trying to get to Coffey."

"Charley Beaumont," Slocum said. "Man back there

said the one on the mule had a beard. That's Charley."
He was listening hard now, but the rush of the creek
drowned out any sound fainter than its own. Fog hov-
ered in the trees up the ravine, where after a hundred
yards the trail disappeared in the gloom. "What's up
that way?"

"Hobbs' place is about ten miles up. Chilly Wind
Pass maybe two days' ride beyond that. Chilly Wind's
the only way across those mountains. First good snow
could close it. Could be they aim to put it between
you and them."

"I doubt it. I know Hobbs' kind. Walker's kin to
him. Push comes to shove, he'll take him in. Likely
Walker's done some heavy talking so Hobbs'll take
Quinn and Foley, too."

"Well, you got 'em running, anyway. That's something."

"Charley's running too far. These other three'll
keep. Let's head for the Coffey road." He mounted
up, reined the bay around, and headed down the trail
at a lope.

He stayed ahead of Ganning again, that eager viciousness still driving him on, so strong he could feel
the heat of it just back of his eyes. Not something
he'd ever thought he would feel toward Charley Beaumont. Charley had always been an amiable sort, able
to keep a whole barroom laughing at his jokes, as
changeable and funny as an actor on a stage. Though
Slocum had known Quinn longer, Charley was in
many ways closer, somebody he'd always trusted.
That had begun to change even before they'd split
sides in Jackson County. Looked at close, what made
Charley so easy-going wasn't pretty to see. He didn't
have much spine, and he'd learned to make people

laugh so he could stay on their good side. Once you saw that clear, it kind of made your skin crawl.

The thing that made him likable—that willingness to go along—was doubtless the very thing that had kept Charley from saying no when whoever it was had gone after Anne. That thought brought bile to Slocum's throat. He closed his mind to any thinking at all.

It was another two hours before they hooked up with the road. By then they were already five miles east of the Hole, and the timber was beginning to thin on the small hills rolling toward Coffey. Still in the lead, the bay moving now at a fast trot, Slocum turned east along the edge of the timber, standing in the stirrups to get a look out onto the road. The tracks of the mule were plain as day, so fresh they looked to be still filling up with water. He turned to give Ganning the high sign and slowed the bay a little, keeping it on thick pine needles under the trees to dampen sound.

They had covered maybe half a mile when he caught sight of Charley. The bay had caught some of his eagerness and was wanting to run. He had to fight it to a halt just inside the trees, and while it danced and fishtailed under him he kept his eyes on the mule heading away from him, fifty yards up the road. The fire was churning in his gut, so strong it was making him sick.

Charley's mule was very small, barely bigger than a burro. There was a large pack lashed on behind its saddle—bedroll and bag and what looked to be a prospector's kit, pickaxe and shovel handle visible even from here. Charley was slumped in the saddle, head down under a floppy hat, and though he could see him only from the back, Slocum could picture the vacant look in his eyes. He had a sudden memory of Charley the way he'd first seen him—gloriously drunk on a Texas beach one sunny afternoon, coming out of the water with his pants legs rolled up, a sultry Mexican girl on one arm, a bottle in his other hand, his beard split wide in a glistening grin. A long time ago.

He became aware that Ganning had brought the roan up beside him. Both horses were lathered from the steady pace. Ganning was watching him, quiet and steady, again waiting like somebody letting a crazy man have his head.

"I want him to myself," Slocum said. "I want to be alone with him."

Ganning studied his eyes. Then he nodded, touched a hand to his hat, and reined the roan back the way they had come.

Slocum waited till he was out of sight. Then he reined south into the trees, aiming to circle wide and come at Charley from the front.

When he figured he was a quarter mile ahead of the mule, he cut back through the timber. He halted at the treeline just long enough to see the road was clear. Then he spurred out onto the mud, in a low spot between two little hills. He put the bay in the center of the road facing west, unbuttoned his sheep-skin, and tucked the skirts of it back to put his Colt within reach. Then he crossed his hands on the sad-dlehorn and waited.

The little mule came over the rise five minutes later, delicate hooves lifting out of the mud like maybe it was moving on tiptoe. Charley had his head down, brooding about something under that floppy hat, and at first he didn't see. Then the bay started acting up again, tossing its head and fighting the reins, and the mule shied toward the side of the road.

Charley's head came up. His coat was open to reveal a handgun stuck in his waistband, but he didn't reach for it. He was so close Slocum could see half a dozen emotions flicker across his face. By the time he got the mule stopped, they were scarcely twenty yards apart.

The bay snorted and shook its mane, setting the bridle chains to jingling. Slocum ignored it.

"Hello, Charley."

"'Lo, John." Charley licked his lips and swallowed, like maybe there was something in his throat he had to get out. "Heard you was in the Hole somewheres." He tried a shaky grin, but it didn't come off too well. "I'm heading out. Decided I was keeping bad company."

"Little late for that, Charley."

Slocum felt heat building up back of his eyes. The anger was so strong in him he had to curb the urge to ride the bay right into the mule, knock the mule over, and throw Charley to the ground. Sensing his impatience, the bay snorted and started sidestepping through the mud, tossing its head, eager to move. Slocum fought it to a standstill, keeping his eyes on Charley.

"You're coming down in the world, Charley. First time I ever seen you riding a mule."

Charley flushed. "Horse went lame. Mule here was all I could afford. Bought it off a prospector. Bought all his gear, too. Thought I might try myself a little prospecting."

"Where's your friends, Charley?"

Charley glanced over his shoulder, like maybe afraid they might overhear. "You mean Paul and them?"

"You been running with anybody else lately?" Too itchy to sit still, Slocum let up on the reins. The bay tried to bolt, but he fought it into a tight circle around the mule—once around, and then twice, while Charley sat rigid in the saddle, his face white and that shaky smile still pasted to his face. Slocum forced the bay's nose back almost to his boot to get it to turn and drove it right up alongside the mule, putting them nose to tail. "I want to know where they are, Charley."

"We split up, John. They was aiming to try Hobbs' place." Charley kept that shaky grin on his face, like maybe if he showed himself friendly long enough, nothing bad would happen. "I wouldn't go with 'em. Could have got myself a horse, probably, joining up with Hobbs, but I wouldn't go with 'em. Things ain't been right between us, John. I wanted out."

"You took your time about it. And you didn't come tell me where they'd gone, now, did you? You could have come looking for me, Charley. You could have left word at Bushnell's."

"I aimed to, John. I aimed to. But I couldn't bring myself to do it. I was scared. I been real scared, John."

"You never could bring yourself to do anything, could you, Charley? You always needed somebody telling you what to do and when to do it." Slocum sent the restless bay through that tight circle again, watching Charley freeze when he passed behind him. Then he fought the bay back up alongside the mule, where it chewed the bit and sawed at the reins. "Who was it told you what to do back in Jackson County, Charley? Whose idea was that?"

"Wasn't nobody's idea, John." Charley sneaked a

glance at the way Slocum's coattail was peeled back
to expose his Colt. "Was an accident. I swear 'fore
God it was an accident."

"Don't insult me, Charley. I'm going to kill you
anyway. Don't make it worse."

"God, John, don't. I didn't have nothing to do with
it. I swear I didn't."

Slocum spurred the bay into the mule, slamming
its forequarters into the mule's flanks. "Tell me who
did it, Charley."

"I don't know, John. I don't know." Charley worked
to keep the mule steady. "We was drunk. I don't know
who did it."

Slocum slammed the bay into the mule again. "Tell
me, Charley."

"John, I don't know. We'd been drinking all day.
Somebody said we ought to ride out and talk to you.
Bob, I think. Only you wasn't there. She was there
alone, and I guess that's why it happened."

Slocum couldn't hold still. He raked the bay with
his spurs and fought it around that tight muddy circle
again, feeling it straining at the reins, wanting to run.
He kept it moving, needing the effort just to work off
his own heat. Every time he passed behind the mule
Charley seemed to freeze, as if afraid his turning around
would somehow make Slocum madder than he was,
and every time he circled back to the front Charley's
eyes picked him up from the side and followed him
around, eyeing the Colt still in the holster. And all
the while Charley kept on talking, words spilling out
like maybe if he told it fast enough and right enough
he wouldn't have to die.

"We was only going to talk, John. 'Fore God,
nobody had it in mind to do anything like that. And

I was drunk, John. I don't remember it too well. First thing I knew, we was in that room, with Anne there naked in the tub. Don't remember who it was got her out of there. Frank, I think. We was all of us drunk, see. It just happened. All of them jumping her. But I didn't touch her, John. I swear 'fore God, I didn't touch her. You know I couldn't have done a thing like that."

Slocum kept the bay restlessly circling. "Why'd you kill her, Charley? Raping her was one thing. Why'd you have to kill her, too?"

"I told you, John, it was an accident. I didn't see it. I seen things getting out of hand and I went outside. Tell you the truth, John, I was sick. Puking up my guts back of the house."

Slocum fought the bay up alongside the mule and leaned to put his eyes up close to Charley's, watching Charley blanch at what he saw there. "Who killed her, Charley?"

"John, I don't know."

Charley was near to crying now, but Slocum was too angry to feel anything except the steaming heat just back of his eyes. He circled the bay around the mule again and lashed Charley across the face with the ends of his reins.

"Who killed her, Charley?"

Charley flinched and raised a hand to shield his face. "John, they wouldn't say. Wouldn't nobody talk about it after that. Won't nobody talk about nothing anymore."

Slocum circled the mule again. He believed him. That would be the way the others would treat Charley.

Edgy and angry, he kept the bay moving at an awkward trot, the horse white-eyed and fighting the bit and trying all the time to bolt. "Get down off that mule, Charley. I'm going to kill you, and I want you facing me with a gun in your hand when I do."

"John, I swear I never touched her. I didn't even watch. I didn't have nothing to do with killing her, John. I don't even know who did. John, you can't do this."

Slocum lashed at him with the reins again. "You were my friend, Charley, and a friend don't do what you done. Now I'm going to kill you. Get down off that mule."

"John, I can't." Charley had his head turned away behind that upraised hand. "You know I can't, John. I can't do that."

Slocum hit him with the reins from the other side. "Get down off that mule, Charley."

Charley flinched. "Why, John? Why? You know I didn't touch her."

"Because you didn't have the guts to try and stop 'em. You didn't have the guts to cut 'em loose later. You didn't have the guts to come tell me what they'd done. Because you *got* no guts, Charley. You're a crawling, cringing sneak, and you make me sick."

Charley wiped his nose on his sleeve. "John, don't talk to me like that."

"You been eating away at my gut a long time, Charley, you and them others, and I'm tired of being sick. I used to think you were a man. All the time you were just sucking up to me 'cause you were scared of me. You got one chance left to be a man, Charley. Get off that mule."

"John, it wasn't sucking up. You was my friend, John. Hell, you was the only friend I ever had."

Still circling the mule, Slocum lashed him with the

reins again. "You yellow-bellied sneak, get off that mule."

"John, please don't talk to me like that."

Slocum hit him again. "I'm tired of looking at you, Charley. You make me want to spit."

"Don't talk to me like that, John."

"I'll kill you on your knees if I have to, Charley. Maybe that's where you'd like it. That's where you lived most of your life, ain't it?"

Charley was glaring at him, eyes red-rimmed and wet. "John, I said don't talk to me like that."

Slocum kicked the bay up closer and hit him with the reins. "You spineless woman, get down and draw on me."

Charley let out something between a bleat and a whimper and grabbed for Slocum's reins. The mule shied, and Slocum spurred the bay into that tight circle again. Even as he moved, he saw Charley clawing at the Colt in his belt.

The first shot came when he was still to Charley's rear. Pasty-faced, swearing a blue streak, Charley had hauled the Colt out and swivelled in the saddle, snapping off a shot so desperate it came near clipping the bay's ears. The horse squealed and hunched and started to buck, crow-hopping around to put Slocum's back to the mule. A second shot sang past, and the bay squealed again and tried to lurch away; Slocum fought it around in time to see Charley had the mule turned and was aiming the Colt at arm's length, still swearing a blue streak. A third shot plucked at Slocum's hatbrim, and then his own Colt was up and out and bucking in his hand.

The shot lifted Charley half out of the saddle. The mule shied and slipped and almost went down in the mud, flinging Charley down to grab for a handhold around its neck. Ears laid back, the mule trotted a dozen yards off the road and came to a halt in the patchy trees, Charley still sprawled down across its withers, his arms hung up in the reins he'd had knotted over the saddlehorn. He wasn't moving. His Colt lay where he'd dropped it in the mud of the road. And now blood began dripping from the fingers of one dangling hand.

# 9

Slocum fought the bay to a standstill in the middle of the road. He was surprised to find his hands shaking. He could feel his lungs laboring in his ribcage, and still he couldn't seem to get enough air. He holstered his Colt, braced his hands on the saddlehorn, and sucked in breath till something like a chill rippled through him and he could breathe again. The bay stamped and shifted nervously under him. When he was sure he had himself pulled together, he let up on the reins and walked the horse off the road.

The mule still stood patiently in the trees, Charley's body sprawled down across its neck. Blood was dripping off the one hand hanging lower than the other, steady enough to pool up on the ground. He was glad the head hung down the other side so he couldn't see the face; Charley's face wasn't something he particularly wanted to see. Without giving himself time to think about it, he dismounted and untangled the arms from the knotted reins and lowered the body to the ground.

Charley's belly was a mass of blood, and his face was as gray as his beard. The eyes weren't quite closed, and the mouth sagged open. Slocum retrieved the floppy hat from where it had fallen on the road and covered Charley's face with it. Then he hunkered down beside the body, feeling that chill ripple through

him again. Trying to steady his hands, he pulled out
a sack of Golden Grain and began rolling up a smoke.

He couldn't bring himself to think. His hands were
still shaking so bad he spilled the tobacco and tore
the paper before he could get it rolled. He swore and
tossed it away and fished another paper from his vest
pocket; he was hungry for something strong in his
lungs. He forced himself to concentrate, and this time
he got the thing crimped and rolled and twisted up
tight. He touched a match to it and sucked in as much
as he could hold and let himself look at Charley's
body.

With the face covered, he didn't have to acknowl-
edge that that was Charley under there, and he still
couldn't make himself think. Not about what it was
he'd just done. All he could put his mind on was how
dead a dead man looked. Something in the way the
body lay on the ground, unnaturally heavy and motionless, nothing alive inside. Nothing but a slab of
meat. The bloody part looked like something off a
carving block. He didn't want to think of Charley like
that, and he turned his eyes away.

He hung the cigarette from the corner of his mouth
and put his hands out where he could look at them.
The shaking was gone. All that remained was the
slowly receding anger that had caused them to shake
in the first place, and now that it was receding he
could begin to separate out what it was he was angry
at: at Charley, for what he had done and what he
hadn't done; at life, for making Charley what he was,
so that this had had to come to pass; and at himself,
for pushing into a showdown a man whom he'd thought
was a good and loyal friend, who had likely told the
truth about what had happened back in Texas, and

who had had very little chance against him here, no
matter what the odds. To keep from thinking about
that, he got up and took a pick and shovel from the
pack the mule was carrying and set about digging a
grave.

He had dug down about a foot in the muddy ground
when he heard a horse approaching and turned to see
Ganning walking the roan through the trees toward
him. Ganning was watching the ground in front of his
horse, nothing much showing on his face. He pulled
up a few yards away, tilted his hat back, and looked
from Slocum to the body on the ground.

"He had his chance," Slocum said.

"I know," Ganning said. "I was back over there a
ways watching."

The drizzle had stopped. The roan snorted and shook
its mane. Ganning dismounted with a creak of saddle
leather and bent to lift the hat from Charley's face.

"Yeah, I've seen him. One of the ones I seen in
Bushnell's. He tell you what you needed to know?
Which one it was killed her?"

"No. Claimed he was too drunk. Said he was outside heaving up his guts when it happened, and the
rest of 'em wouldn't talk about it."

"You believe that?"

"I believe it. That's about where Charley would be
at a time like that. And they wouldn't tell him. Not
unless he pushed. And Charley wasn't the kind to
push."

Ganning replaced the hat and straightened up. "Kind
of leaves you where you were, then, don't it?"

"Not exactly. You think I was wrong? You think
I should have handled this different?"

"Not my place to say." Ganning reached for the

pick. "Better get him in the ground before it starts raining again."

They got the grave about three feet deep before the hole began filling up with water. Slocum called it off then and hauled Charley's bedroll off the mule and rolled the body in it, and together he and Ganning lowered it in. He took his hat off then, for lack of anything better to do, and stood looking down at the bundle in the grave. It didn't look like much—not like anything he could think of as Charley Beaumont—and his mind had gone blank on him again. He didn't know much about Charley's growing up, whether he had a family anywhere or whether it would matter to anybody else that Charley was dead. Ganning had taken his own hat off and was standing at the other end of the hole, waiting. His silence was making Slocum uncomfortable. Somebody maybe ought to say something, but he could never think of anything to say at a time like this.

The ground water had begun to seep up into the bedroll, turning the edges of it wet and dark. And now it started drizzling again, rain pelting softly on the fresh earth piled up beside the grave.

"You want me to leave you with him?" Ganning said.

Slocum put his hat back on. "I got no words to say over this grave. I did what I had to do." He picked up the shovel then and without looking into the hole again started shoveling in the mud and dirt that had come out of it.

When he was finished, he thrust the shovel into the ground at the head of the grave and hung Charley's floppy hat on the handle. That would have to do for a grave marker. It wouldn't be the first nameless roadside grave in this country. He raked some of the mud off his boots with his spurs and led the mule over toward where he'd tethered the bay.

"Feel better now?" Ganning said.

"No, I can't say I do. But I will. When I've got 'em all, I will."

"He say where they'd gone?"

"Said they were aiming to try Hobbs' place." He tied the mule's reins to his saddlestrings and swung up onto the bay. "Evidently Walker changed Hobbs' mind about taking them in."

"If he has, you've lost them. No way you can get to them up there."

"I'll get to 'em. I don't care what it takes. Come on. Let's get away from here." He clucked to the bay then and headed for the road, the mule plodding along behind.

The drizzle had stopped again by the time they reached the edge of Hobbs' Hole, but the sky was still as dark as the first day he'd seen it, and Bushnell's was showing lamplight in the windows. Slocum was in the lead—Ganning had hung back the whole time, as if to leave him alone with his thoughts—and now he reined up at the brow of the hill where the road sloped down to make the run to Bushnell's and waited till Ganning had pulled up beside him.

"Where's Hobbs' place from here?"

Ganning nodded toward the heavily timbered ridges far across on the other side of the Hole. "About due west of Bushnell's. Place called Hobbs' Pocket. Another flat valley like the Hole, only smaller. Maybe ten miles up in that timber."

"He's got family up there?"

"Wife and kids, but the boys are grown. It ain't

family you got to worry about. If that's where they've gone, you better give it up."

"I don't care if it's God himself sheltering them. I ain't giving it up." Slocum leaned back to loose the mule's reins from his saddlestrings. "You going past Bushnell's?"

"I can if there's reason to."

"I'd be obliged if you'd take this mule down there. Tell Bushnell you found it back there by that fresh-dug grave. Bushnell will get word to them."

Ganning took the reins from him. "You think that'll flush them out?"

"I just want them to know Charley didn't make it, that I'm still here, and not fixing to leave. I want to make it a little harder for them to sleep nights."

Ganning shrugged. "If you say so. I doubt it'll make them move out of there."

"Just tell Bushnell about that fresh grave. I'll worry about the rest of it."

Ganning clucked to the roan and started down the muddy road toward Bushnell's, leading the mule behind him. Slocum stayed where he was, scanning those timbered ridges climbing west up out of the Hole. Up in there somewhere were Quinn and Foley and Walker, settling down to ride out the winter, in the place called Hobbs' Pocket. Maybe ten miles up, Ganning had said. He could see nothing but the dark of the timber, one ridge rising behind the other toward the higher range of mountains beyond, where the line of Chilly Wind Pass cut through peaks already white with snow. He doubted they would try to make it across there. Not so long as they felt safe in Hobbs' Pocket. But maybe they weren't as safe as they thought they were. There was more than one way to flush grouse out of a thicket.

He turned the bay and started back along the road toward the cut-off to the shack. He needed a drink. He had a feeling he was going to need to get drunk. Drunk enough to pass out, so he wouldn't have to think about what he'd done to Charley Beaumont.

# 10

He was coming up through the trees from the road
when he saw his packhorse, still wearing its halter,
tethered near the back of the shack. The door to the
shack stood open, and a homemade broom he hadn't
seen before was leaning against an outside wall. The
packhorse was loaded with gear, two gunny sacks full
of stuff knotted astraddle of its withers and a large
pack lashed down across its rump. Fixed to its halter
was a single rein fashioned from a length of rope.
From the look of things, Susan had gone off somewhere and brought back supplies—more supplies than
he figured they needed.

She came to the door when he reined the bay up
outside. She had her sleeves rolled up and a dust rag
in one hand. Her hair was bound up under a scarf,
and he could see by the sweat along her hairline that
she'd been working hard. She didn't say anything,
but the look on her face said she was expecting him
to give her trouble. He stepped past her for a look
inside.

She had taken the blanket down. The rope he'd
strung across the room to hang the blanket on was
gone. Some pots and pans he hadn't seen before were
stacked near the hearth, and on the table was an oil
lamp to replace the candles. The place looked as
spruced up as any he'd ever been in, like maybe she'd

not only swept it but scrubbed it clean. And in the corner where her bedroll had been she'd set up an iron-railed bedframe, with some weathered boards for slats and the blanket draped neatly over the railing at the head of it.

He turned to find her still in the doorway. "Where'd you get it?"

"In that pile of boards where the barn was." She was watching him warily. "There's no springs to it, but we can sleep on it. I've slept on worse."

"I don't recall saying I would share a bed with you."

She flushed. "I never noticed you turning me down them times after the candle's out. And, anyway, you can sleep on the floor if you want. I want me a bed." She wiped her hands on the dust rag then and went to pick through the pots by the hearth, separating them out by size.

He propped the Greener in a corner and draped his slicker over the back of a chair. "You hadn't ought to be riding around out there by yourself. There's men here could be dangerous to you." When he had his sheepskin off, he fished in his bag for a box of cheroots. She had rolled his bedroll up neatly and laid it across the foot of the bed, along with her own, and the oil lamp was already lit, adding its warm glow to the daylight coming in the door. One thing she hadn't changed: his whiskey bottle and glass still stood where he'd left them on the table. He poured himself three fingers' worth and downed half of it. "Where'd you get the money for all this? I ain't paying any credit at Bushnell's."

"I didn't get it at Bushnell's. Tom Price made me the loan of it."

"You didn't tell me you knew Tom Price."

"You didn't ask. He gave me a featherbed we can use for a mattress, too." She straightened up and wiped a sleeve across her brow. "It's still out there on the horse. I'd be obliged if you'd help me bring that stuff in."

"You're aiming to set up housekeeping, are you?"

"We've already set up housekeeping. You may not like it, but that's what we've done. I'm just trying to make it comfortable."

He drank off the whiskey. "Don't try so hard. It ain't worth your time."

"It's my time," she said. "I'll do what I want with it."

That night he sat alone at the table with the bottle and his glass, brooding at the picture stuck in the mirror on the wall. Susan had cleared the dishes away after supper and washed them in the iron pot she used for heating water over the fire. They had said very little all through supper, and he was glad of that. He hadn't told her about Charley Beaumont. He was trying not to think about Charley Beaumont.

He could hear her moving around behind him now, fixing and straightening and putting things right. She had already spent an hour chinking cracks around the windows with scraps of hide she'd got from Tom Price, trying to close the cold out. Likely she was aiming to make the shack snug for winter, but he had no intention of spending the winter with her here, no matter what she had in mind.

He figured all this wifely work was designed to impress him—that, and the way she kept making a display of that astonishing body of hers. The fire in the fireplace was heating the room up good, and after a while she'd stripped off the shirtwaist she'd worn tucked into her skirt, working then in whatever that thin garment was she had on under it, so skimpy she was virtually naked from the waist up. Maybe she figured it didn't matter after all the times she'd crept out to his bedroll those nights in front of the fire, but she couldn't know what it did to him to see her like that.

He couldn't look at her without seeing Anne, without remembering Anne doing those same wifely chores in that house back in Texas, couldn't see her breasts moving big and heavy under that thin garment without remembering how it had been to slide beneath cool sheets and find Anne waiting for him there, soft and warm and eager, and her body slim and supple and naked when he pulled back the blankets to take her all in at once. He couldn't remember that without seeing that same body sprawled dead and bloody on the floor where they'd left her.

It had been a good thing to have his own woman after all those years alone on the trail. A woman he believed in and trusted to stick by him, a woman he was willing to stay in one place for. By the time he'd met her, he had long since come to believe that was something he was never going to have.

A man put down roots when he found a woman like Anne. Having those roots ruptured left some pretty big wounds, and the wounds weren't healed yet. He figured they weren't likely to heal till he'd done away with the cause of them: Frank Walker, Bob Foley, and Paul Quinn. What was left of the men in that picture on the wall, now that Charley Beaumont was dead.

He could see Charley looking at him from the picture. He tried to remember Charley the night that picture was taken—something good to put his mind on, some memory of a better time, because he remembered they'd had a good time that night—but all he could think of was Charley, pasty-faced and scared out there on the road, gone all mealy-mouthed with the fear that was in him, sitting astraddle of a mule like some yellow-bellied sodbuster who'd never had the guts to do anything but follow a plow, hiding behind the skirts of his woman and breeding kids like maybe that would prove his manhood, spreading out across what had once been good country with others of his kind, like locusts swarming myriad and mindless across the sky. He had met some sodbusters in his time who were good men, but as a general rule he found them spineless. He didn't like to admit that Charley had been as spineless as any of them.

He'd been nursing his whiskey for over an hour when he heard Susan moving around in the corner behind him, making more noise than she needed to. Likely she was annoyed that all this fixing and cleaning hadn't got the response she'd hoped for. Or maybe she was just tired of looking at his back. He didn't want to deal with her now.

After a while she said, "You'll burn a hole in that picture, you keep looking at it like that."

He turned to see her watching him from the bed. While he'd been sitting there, she'd spread the featherbed out on the slats for a mattress, laid both bedrolls on top of that and covered the whole thing with a bear robe she'd borrowed from Price. She was perched on the edge of the bed now, and all she had on was that skimpy little shift she'd been wearing to sleep in.

"Please come to bed," she said. "All that drinking isn't going to help."

He could tell she had posed herself there special. Her breasts were so big they lifted that little shift up like a tent, so that it scarcely reached her shapely thighs. Her bare legs slanted down just so, and one little arm lay along the rail at the head of the bed. She looked apprehensive but determined, and for an instant he was impressed with her nerve.

He cut that feeling off sharp, but he curbed his anger. "You go on to sleep," he said. "I'll be along directly." And he turned back away from her.

He heard her sigh and then the creak of the bed as she moved. He poured himself another drink and went back to brooding at the picture.

Again he tried to remember something good about Charley, something to erase the memory of Charley scared and shaking on the mule out there on the road, but he couldn't get his mind to move beyond that, couldn't shake the sight of Charley's face when he'd crested the muddy hill and seen the bay waiting for him there in the road, couldn't shake the sight of Charley trying to grin, hoping maybe the old humor would get him out of what he had to know was a spot he was never going to get out of alive. The sight of that was like a blind pulled down across the back of his eyes, so he couldn't remember Charley any other way, and if he kept thinking about that he was going to drink himself silly for sure.

But putting that memory out of his mind didn't help, because that left him alone with the picture on the wall, and Charley seemed to be looking right at him. He figured the whiskey was beginning to work in him now, because he couldn't shake the feeling that Charley was alive up there, looking at him with a grin that seemed to grow weaker and shakier with every minute, like maybe Charley was still pleading for his life, or had maybe come back to haunt him, and would keep on haunting him so long as that picture was there where he could see it. And where Charley could see him.

He tried to pull himself together and see the picture clear, but that just made things worse, because it looked a hell of a lot clearer than any picture had a right to, and he had the feeling Charley's eyes were getting brighter and more alive, so alive they seemed ready to burn holes in the paper they were fixed on. And then Charley's face seemed to change, dissolving into some blurred white shape that gradually revealed itself to be a skull—gleaming white bone with nothing but black holes where the eyes had been and with teeth bared now into one huge glistening grin—and he didn't care if it was only the whiskey working on his mind, he didn't want to look at that skull, and he got up from the table and crossed the room and tore Charley's picture off the edge of the rest, and carried it to the hearth, and threw it in the fire.

For an instant it lay across a log, whole and clear as a desert floor in bright sunlight: Charley Beaumont, bearded and runty and grinning like a fool, one boot propped on a chair so he could display both sixgun and Winchester across his knee, a lot younger then, with less gray in his beard and a lot more fire in his grin. Then the flames licked up around all four edges, the picture seemed to shrink and squirm, and Charley disappeared in a slow wave of heat that turned the paper brown for an instant before it shrivelled and curled up on itself and became only a thin crinkle of ash turning white in the coals.

"Does that mean what I think it means?"

He turned to see Susan propped against the head

of the bed, the bear robe pulled up across her lap, breasts swelling out that skimpy shift.

"I thought you'd gone to sleep," he said.

"I was waiting for you. And you didn't answer my question."

He went back to the table, put the cork in the whiskey bottle, and turned down the wick till the lamp went out. In the flare of firelight he could see a wary look on her face as he came to sit on the edge of the bed and pull his boots off.

"You killed one of them today, didn't you?" she said. "The one in that picture you threw in the fire."

"Never you mind what I did today."

"It ain't pleasant to watch," she said. "What you're doing to yourself, I mean. I can see it happening right in front of me. Like I watched it happen last spring. You killed that man today, and you been sitting there all night trying to forget you done it."

He stood up and started unbuttoning his shirt. "Just because your friend Jesse got himself killed last spring don't mean I'm going to. And if you want to help me forget what happened today, you can take that thing off you got on."

She watched him shuck the rest of his clothes, studying his face as if to see whether it was safe or not. Then she grasped the hem of the shift and pulled it off over her head.

There was fear on her face as she looked at him, but he couldn't take his eyes off her breasts. Seeing that, she arched her back a bit, looking down at herself. He could see her breathing quicken, but he sensed it was fear that was doing it. He didn't care. The sight of her large young breasts suspended above the arch of her ribcage, the supple waist, the smooth slope of flesh curving down under the bear robe had brought up in him again that heat and pressure pulsing in his brain, anger all mixed in where he wasn't used to feeling it, and he yanked the bear robe down and joined her on the bed and pulled her to him.

A little gasp escaped her throat as he entered her. He went all the way in, heat suddenly so strong he closed his arms around her like a vise, crushing her in against him, holding her there, trying to still the sudden violence surging up inside. Slowly she pulled her head back to look at him with slitted eyes, one sleek, warm thigh sliding up across his.

"Does it always have to be angry?" she said.

"Don't talk."

He grasped the hair at the nape of her neck and held her head in place. He wanted to see the fear on her face. The pull on her hair caused her eyes to slit even more; he could feel her fingers clinging desperately to his arms. The look on her face was that of a cornered animal, but she was warm and wet and trembling with something more than fear.

"You want it to be angry," she said.

"I don't want to talk," he said, and retracted just enough to give him leverage and thrust violently into her, so hard he could feel bone meeting bone.

He lost himself then. The whiskey fuming through his blood took over, and he had no control anymore. They became only wild and heated movement, and only snatches of it reached his brain: him on his knees driving into her so violently she had to grasp the bedrail behind her, her huge breasts wobbling with the force of his thrusts; her body arching up off the bed as she gripped the bedrail, her head going back and her eyes closed; the one time she rose up in re-

sistance and tried to twist away and the sudden gasp
that came from her when he slapped her and forced
her back in rhythm, and the new and explosive writh-
ing of her body when he did so; the feel of her belly
slapping and sliding against his and the frantic high
cries that pierced the silence when she came, bringing
him over after her. And then the long shuddering that
rippled through them after, slowly subsiding into quiet,
stillness, a silence that made him fully aware again,
aware of the separateness of her, and of himself.

For a long time neither of them moved. He could
feel her breasts against his chest when she breathed.
He couldn't see her face, and he sensed she wanted
it that way. Soon he felt something cold come into
the pit of his stomach, and it was all he could do not
to shove her away. He could tell she felt it, too—
some change in the set of his body, in the way he lay
against her. The heat was rapidly draining from the
surface of her skin, as if whatever that cold thing was
had got hold of her, too.

After a while, she pulled back away from him. For
a long time she regarded him with distantly hostile
eyes. Once she started to say something, then thought
better of it. Finally, she said, "You do want it to be
angry."

He pulled away then and lay on his back and looked
at the ceiling. Light from the fire in the fireplace
flickered across the room. He was trying to get his
mind to work, but nothing would come.

"You want it to be angry," she said. "Long as you
stay angry, you won't let yourself go again. Like you
did with her."

"I told you, I don't want to talk."

"That's part of it, too. If we talked some, we might

get to know each other. You couldn't risk that, could you." When he didn't answer, she said, "You're so angry it's burning you up inside."

He reached for the bear robe and pulled it up over him. "They're my insides. I don't need you to tell me they're burning up."

"It won't help killing them. You killed one of them today. You don't seem any less angry for it."

"There's three of them left. I'll breathe easy when they're dead, too."

She was silent for a long while. After a while he felt her hand come over to touch his arm, rest there a bit, then go away. "You must have been a nice man once," she said. "There's no other man in Hobbs' Hole who would have defended me in Bushnell's. 'Cept maybe Will Ganning or Tom Price."

"Why don't you go hole up with them, then. Why waste your time with me?"

"It's my time," she said. "I'll do what I want with it."

Long after she was asleep he lay awake in the dark, remembering what it had been like to share a bed with Anne, remembering what it had been like to come home and find her dead on the floor, remembering Charley Beaumont, pasty-faced and scared, out there on the road. Through the dark he sensed the remnant of that picture on the wall across the room, the two men pictured there, and the one who was not, somewhere up in the hills now, west of the Hole, waiting.

# 11

Every sunrise of the next six days found him waiting
and watching in the timber above Hobbs' Pocket.

The weather had turned. The rain had stopped, and
the nights began to turn cold and the dawns chilly.
Every morning before daybreak he would follow a
well-worn trail west up out of the Hole till the timber
ceased, then circle around onto this ridge, putting the
mountains and the snow-covered peaks of Chilly Wind
Pass at his back because he wanted a vantage point
down into the Pocket.

The Pocket was a good ten miles above the Hole
and maybe a fifth the size, flat as a lake bed, half of
it in pasture, half in grain, the fields turned to stubble
now the harvest was in, and set like a gem in the
middle of it was the kind of place a Southerner like
Hobbs would have even here: a tall and many-gabled
white house with open verandas along both stories.
There was a shed or two in a vegetable garden out
back; to the left of the house was a big bunkhouse
and maybe fifty yards to the right a barn built like the
house, not of log but of slab lumber. Somewhere down
in that Pocket, in one of those buildings, were the rest
of the men he'd been hunting for a good part of a
year now.

The bunkhouse occupied his attention the first day.
It was a single-story structure, built of log and set off

to the left of the house, near a cluster of sheds he took to be a smokehouse and a henhouse with a fenced-in chicken run and what was likely an icehouse solid-built in the midst of the others. For one whole day he watched every man who entered or left that bunk-house, and though he counted a dozen different men, there wasn't one he recognized, and not even one he could believe might be Frank Walker. Increasingly after that he focussed on the house itself, some inner instinct telling him that was where Hobbs would house his kin, even unwelcome kin like Walker, even with the two or three strangers that couldn't be called kin. So he would make his way to this vantage point every morning in the dark, tie the bay to a tree, and hunker down against another, waiting patiently with his field glasses for the sun to come up, ready with a patience born of months on the trail to study that house till darkness fell again.

Dawn broke every morning in a thin, pale line across the horizon to the east, and simultaneously with the dawn would come the flicker and flare of an oil lamp in a first-floor window, the rest of the house still nothing but a remembered shape in the darkness. He would watch as the light receded away, the window fading back into night as whoever was carrying the lamp left the room and closed the door. Soon he would see another faintly lighted window take shape in the dark, and then another, and another as the lamp was carried toward what eventually proved to be a stair-case, and then he would see that steadily growing light dawn in a second-story window as the lamp slowly ascended the stairs.

That window likely opened on a hall, because no sooner had it taken shape in the dark than it would blink out, the light flaring simultaneously alive in a second window beside the first, in a room he took to be a bedroom, where the lamp would settle and remain still and gradually grow pale while dawn broke slowly over the Pocket, laying bare to the cold winter sun the house and the sheds and the barn and the horses in the corral to the south of the barn.

Every day would begin the same. The lamp would leap to life and make its errant passage through the house. The sun would crack the crooked hills to the east, and dawn would widen slowly across all the country he could see. And he would wait. Twenty minutes would pass. Then thirty. Then forty. Then the sharp clap of a door would break the brittle air and Hobbs would emerge onto the ground-floor veranda, bundled in sheepskin and gloves, a scarf bound around his Stetson to keep his ears warm, and make his way along the path behind the house. Slocum would put the glasses on him, following him along the path, watching the white wisps of breath vanish into the air behind him till the man himself disappeared into the barn.

Hobbs always seemed the first one up. Slocum figured it was him carrying the lamp to the upstairs bedroom, likely checking on that boy of his that was hurt, and it wasn't till the clap of the door came that he saw any other sign of life within the house. And the mornings never varied. First Hobbs would make that lamplit pilgrimage along the hall and up the stairs, and after exactly forty minutes he would emerge into the cold and frosty morning to spend another hour doing whatever it was he found to do there in the barn.

"I figure he's admiring that prize bull of his," Ganning said when Slocum told him about it. "I watched up there a week or two myself, trying to get a sense of the place. Getting that bull's put the cap on Hobbs' little personal Reconstruction. He's made himself the kind of landowner he was in Tennessee before the War. Now he wants his sons to live respectable."

"Too late for that from what I've seen," Slocum said. "And if he wants 'em to live at all, he better stop sheltering that Jackson County bunch. I have to fight my way in there, I may just kill his sons."

So far he had seen no sign of what he had come to think of as the Jackson County bunch. After the first day he decided they weren't bedded down in the bunkhouse with the crew, and he hadn't seen them anywhere around the big house. By the evening of the second day he was beginning to think maybe Ganning was right. Maybe they'd decided to put Chilly Wind Pass behind them. He hated to think of them moving down into the country on the other side, wild country where it would be hard to track them. And then, late in the afternoon of the third day, he caught his first sight of them.

At first he didn't realize it was them. He'd had his field glasses on the barn when movement near the house caught his eye. He lowered the glasses and saw two men on the veranda there, one of them pointing up toward the mountains. He put the glasses on them and saw that the man pointing was Hobbs, the other a tall and square-built man he didn't know. This man shaded his eyes to look where Hobbs was pointing, moving his head like maybe he was scanning the very ridge Slocum was sitting on. Then Hobbs said something toward the door they'd come out of, and another man emerged, a man Slocum recognized as Paul Quinn.

Behind Quinn came Bob Foley. The two of them joined Hobbs and the other man, the man who must be Frank Walker, at the veranda rail. They were all looking up toward him, and for a moment he thought they must have seen him. Then, after scanning the hills for a minute or two, all four left the veranda and strolled out into the yard.

Slocum lowered the glasses. He could feel the old heat beating through him, a viciousness so strong it made him feel faint. He put the glasses on them again, watching Hobbs showing them around his garden, pointing at the sheds, talking like the proud landowner Ganning said he was. After a while, all four filed out along the path behind the house, the same path Hobbs took every morning in the chilly dawn, and disappeared into the barn.

Slocum lowered the glasses again. Though he knew it wasn't smart, he wished he had a Sharps big fifty. The Winchester would be no good at this distance, but with a Sharps he just might be able to hit them from here. But likely he could get only one before the others made it to the house, and they could hold him off from there easily and slip away when night fell without him even knowing they were gone—assuming Hobbs' bunch didn't get to him first. Besides, he wanted to be up close when he did it; he wanted to watch their eyes while they died. He would have to do it some other way.

He watched them for the next three days, patient, thoughtful, holding in check the heat that had driven him all the way from Texas. They didn't mingle with the bunkhouse crew, and they never moved very far from the house, and every time they came out they took a good look around before leaving the shelter of the veranda. Likely they had heard about Charley Beaumont by now.

They had to figure Hobbs' Hole wasn't safe for

them, no matter what Hobbs' rules were. They wouldn't show up in Bushnell's for a while. But they would feel safe in that house down there. That house was where he would have to take them.

When he left the Pocket that last evening, he circled around by the south rim of the Hole, coming down on Tom Price's place from the hill behind it. Early twilight was setting in, and the air was cold. There would be snow on the ground before long. He halted in the timber above the clearing, watching a thin trickle of smoke rising from Price's chimney. When he was sure it was safe, he clucked to the bay and rode on in.

The sound of an axe led him off into the trees behind Price's chicken coop. He found Price and Ganning there, cutting firewood. They'd felled a good-sized tree and sectioned half of it with a cross-cut, and Price was lopping limbs off the rest. Ganning had split a length of log with a wedge and had just sunk an axe into it when Slocum dismounted back of the chicken coop.

Ganning wiped the sweat off his face with a kerchief and stuck it back in his pants pocket. "Wondered where you'd been."

"Been up in those hills below Chilly Wind," Slocum said. "Watching things around Hobbs' place."

"Figured that was it. I told you, if they're up there, you can say goodbye to them."

"They're up there. I been watching them for three days now. That's what I want to talk to you about."

"Nothing to talk about. If Hobbs has taken them in, you can't get them out. Simple as that."

Slocum propped a boot on the log and built himself a smoke. He had figured Ganning would say that, but he didn't want to tackle that place alone. Not unless he had to. He gazed off into the twilight, trying to think of some way to change Ganning's mind.

"What about Hobbs' boys? You did say they're why you're here," he said to the deputy.

"I can't do anything against them now. Got nothing on 'em that can be proved. All I can do is wait till they move again. Go out to hit another bank. Or a train."

"Then what'll you do?"

"Nothing here. If I'm lucky, I'll know where they're going, and when. I'll have a force of marshals and deputies waiting there to meet them. Could be those friends of yours might go with them. You want to throw in on that, you're welcome to."

"You got any idea when they might move again?"

"From the sound of things, one of them's dying. And Hobbs is onto them now. Maybe they won't go out. Maybe they won't go out till spring." He seized the axe and pried it out of the log. "You better start laying in some firewood yourself. Going to be a long winter."

Slocum watched Price throw his axe down and come back along the tree toward them. He figured Ganning was right. Winter was setting in, and with Hobbs watching them now and one of their own dying in that upstairs bedroom, those boys wouldn't be going out again. Not before spring, anyway. And even if they did, he doubted Quinn and Foley would go with them. Walker, maybe, but Quinn and Foley were too smart for that.

Price had joined them now, taking his hat off and wiping a sleeve across his brow. "That girl from Bushnell's was over here the other day," he said. "Said she'd tied up with you after she left there. I gave her some supplies 'cause she asked me to, but I can't say I was happy to hear where she was. You taking care of her?"

Slocum flicked his cigarette off into the twilight. He didn't want to think about Susan. "She acts like she can take care of herself."

Price snorted and looked away. Then: "What you planning on doing about her if you take on Hobbs' bunch?"

"She's all right where she is. She's planning on heading for Coffey the next time Bushnell sends his supply wagon out."

Price didn't say anything. After a bit, he spat on the ground and paced back along the downed tree and went to lopping off limbs again.

Ganning scraped his axe head against the log, working the pitch off it. "You take my advice, you'll head for Coffey yourself. 'Less you want to be stuck here all winter. They ain't going to move out of Hobbs' Pocket. No reason why they should."

Slocum stuck a boot in the stirrup and swung up into the saddle. "If they don't move out, I'll move in after them. I didn't come all this way to give it up now." He touched spurs to the bay's flanks then and trotted on up out of the clearing.

Something of what Price had said about Susan stayed with him that night, and he tried to curb the angry aloofness being around her brought up in him. He had one drink during supper, then corked the bottle and put it away. He saw her take note of that, could tell by the look in her eyes that she was judging the meaning of it, but she didn't say anything, and he was glad of that. He didn't want her seeing more meaning in it than was there, but he was tired of the edginess between them. He had enough on his mind without having to fight her, too.

He had to keep a tight rein on himself to check his anger when she doused the lamp and crawled into bed with him. She seemed to sense it; she only laid a hand on his chest and didn't say anything, waiting to follow his lead. After a while the feel of her smooth skin next to his overcame whatever doubts he'd been nursing. He reached for her then, glad to feel the ease with which she rolled in against him, one leg going up over his, opening to give him entry. He lost himself in her then, drowned in her, glad to have her there to take him out of himself, and it was only at the end that the anger surged up in him, bitter anger that he was still what he was and couldn't lose the memory of that other shapely body back in Texas, dead now and turning to dust in its grave.

Neither of them spoke after it was over. He lay awake with his thoughts, like he'd been lying awake in every bed he'd been in for months, thinking about that Jackson County bunch. Only this time it was different. This time they were within his reach. He could get to them. Provided he was willing to ride into Hobbs' Pocket alone, one man against a dozen.

# 12

The room was dead quiet when he woke the next morning. It was long past sunup. He could see light filtering through the skins stretched over the windows. Susan was still asleep, cuddled up against him, sleek and warm and naked under the bear robe. He could feel her breasts swelling against his ribs as she breathed. The wind had stopped sometime during the night, and there was a hush outside, the kind that always came with first snowfall, when the snow seemed to dampen all sound. Then he heard again the sound that had brought him awake: the ring of a shod hoof on ground frozen hard as stone.

He rolled away from Susan as carefully as he could, eased out of bed, and pulled his pants on. He lifted his Colt from the gunbelt draped over the bedrail and moved across the cold floor to crack the deerhide away from the window.

A good six inches had fallen during the night. The sky was a crisp blue now, the sun so bright that the snow was painful to look at. He saw nothing unusual, just trees like black skeletons in the white of the orchard, and the outhouse, gray and leaning, icicles already dripping along its eaves. Then he saw a horse laboring up through the trees from the road. Will Ganning was in the saddle, wearing a sheepskin coat to his knees, with a scarf around his upturned collar

and another tied down across his hat to protect his
ears from the cold. Slocum released the deerhide and
moved to open the door.

Ganning ground-reined the roan under a tree and
came toward the shack, beating his gloved hands together. "You got good ears. I get you out of bed?"

"Sound carries a long way on a morning like this."
Slocum shivered in the cold air and watched a clump
of snow fall from a tree in the orchard. "See we got
the first snowfall."

"Going to be more of it before long. Looks like
this might melt, but we'll have a foot or two on the
ground before the week's out. I got some news for
you. Mind if I come in?"

Slocum glanced toward the bed. Susan was awake,
propped on one elbow, bare to the waist. Her nipples
were erect from the cold. She struggled up to prop
herself against the wall and tucked the blankets around
her breasts. When she was decent, Slocum stepped
back to let Ganning in.

If Ganning was surprised to see her half-naked in
the only bed in the room, he didn't let on. He nodded
and said, "Mornin', Susan," and went to stand by the
hearth as if he might find warmth from dead ashes.

"Let me warm this place up." Slocum replaced the
Colt in its holster, raked the ashes away with a stick
of kindling, and laid some dried leaves on the last of
the embers. "What's this news you got?" he said, and
went to blowing on the leaves.

"I was down in Bushnell's this morning," Ganning
said. "Bushnell wasn't up yet—just Joe, the cook.
Joe said one of your friends was waiting there when
he opened the place up. The one called Foley."

Slocum turned, still in a crouch. Susan was watching him, but he was busy trying to read Ganning's face. "He leave Bushnell's yet?"

"Left the valley. Said he wanted supplies for a two-day ride. Provisions and such. Joe said he loaded up his saddlebags and headed out the road toward Coffey maybe three hours ago."

"Alone?"

"That's what Joe said. Just Foley, with one horse. Carrying only what he could take in his saddlebags."

Smoke was trickling up from the leaves. Slocum fanned a flame alive and laid some kindling across it. When the kindling caught, he stacked two logs on the fire, stood up, and dusted off his hands. It hadn't quite sunk in yet—Bob Foley was on the run.

"He's splitting off from the rest," Ganning said. "Looks like you scared him out."

"Bob don't scare easy," Slocum said. "He's smart, though, smarter than any of them. He knows I ain't going to stop till I get them all. I figure they're breaking up. A thing like they done, after a while couldn't none of them look the others in the eye. Likely Bob was looking for a reason to leave. And the cook says taking only what he could get in his saddlebags?"

"He didn't have a packhorse with him. I figure he's aiming to catch the train out of Coffey. That's the nearest railhead. Snow coming now, he'd be a fool to try making it on past there on horseback. Likely be a blizzard before too long. That wind'll be cutting across those plains out there like a scythe. A man'd freeze to death trying to ride across that country in this weather."

"Well, he ain't a fool, whatever else he is. When's the next train out of Coffey?"

"Tomorrow. Three-forty in the afternoon. One train a week."

"That means I can catch him."

"If that's what you're set on."

"That's what I'm set on. Looks like Walker and Quinn decided to stick with Hobbs. They'll be here when I get back."

"You want me to go with you? Man could use a little help in a thing like that."

"No, but I appreciate the offer." Slocum had pulled a pair of socks on; now he threw on a thick wool shirt and buttoned it up the front. "Like I said, this is a personal thing. I want him, and I want him my way. I'd rather not deal anybody else in."

"Your choice," Ganning said. "I'll leave you to it. Susan, it's good to see you again. Tom told me you'd found shelter. You need anything, you know where to find me."

Slocum accompanied him to the door. Outside, Ganning turned and blew on his hands. He met Slocum's eyes and then glanced away, the way a man did when he wasn't sure of his ground. "Susan's a good woman," he said, too low for her to hear. "I been watching her down there in Bushnell's for months now. Fending off those boys of Hobbs', dealing with Bushnell and his wife. I know it ain't my business, but she looks to be fond of you. You sure you want to go ahead with what you're doing?"

"That's the one thing I am sure of."

"Not often a man gets himself a woman like that. Maybe you ought to let the past be past. 'Stead of getting yourself killed, you could take Susan somewhere and start over. She'd stick to you."

"I ain't going to get myself killed. But likely you're right about Susan. The kind of woman she is. I'd appreciate your looking in on her while I'm gone. See she's all right."

Ganning nodded, not looking at him. "I'll do that," he said. "Keep your back to the wall when you get to Coffey. I'll see you when you get back." Then he went to his horse and mounted up and started down through the trees toward the road.

Slocum closed the door and turned back into the room. Susan was still sitting up in bed, watching him, the bear robe held up tight under her chin. He stripped to the skin again, aware of her eyes on him, and pulled on his long johns and reached for his shirt. He wondered what she was thinking inside that silence.

"When you planning to leave?" she said.

He looked at her: sober face, soft mouth, serious eyes studying his. "Soon as I'm dressed. I want to get him before he can catch that train."

She got out of bed then, the whole length of that shapely body flashing naked till she got a sheet wrapped around her and went to stand by the fire. "You better wait for breakfast. You got time."

"I don't want any breakfast. And in a thing like this a man never knows if he's got enough time. Something could go wrong. My horse could go lame. I want all the time I can get."

He pulled his pants on, watching her shift to get some of the heat on her legs, those remarkable breasts quivering and jiggling heavily. Her nipples were erect from the cold, clear as anything where they poked out that sheet.

She was still studying his face, quiet and sober as she always was, judging his mood. "You're letting those men run your life," she said. "Everything you do is on account of them. You're going to poison yourself inside, you ain't careful."

He stamped his heels down into his boots and

strapped his gunbelt on. "I already been poisoned inside. I'm trying to get the poison out." He pulled his sheepskin on and reached for his hat. "You might fix me something to eat on the road. I'll be back in as soon as I saddle my horse."

Outside, he put the nosebag on the bay and let it eat while he saddled up. He was thinking about Foley on the run, and Walker and Quinn up there at Hobbs'. Knowing he was here was beginning to split them up, cutting one away from the other, breaking up what had passed as friendship for too many years. It pleased him to picture Walker and Quinn up there now, always on the alert, never able to relax, never knowing when he might show up—or where. Waking in the night to the slightest sound thinking it might be him. Wondering every time they stepped outside if he might be sighting on them with a rifle from someplace up in the timber where they couldn't see. Unable to leave for fear they'd end up like Charley Beaumont, rotting in a hole by the road. Unable even to come down to Bushnell's for fear he might be there.

It pleased him to think he was a constant presence in their minds, as they were a constant presence in his—pleased him to think that if, as Susan said, he was letting them run his life, he was certainly running theirs.

When he had the saddle on and the Winchester in its boot under the cinch strap, he led the bay down to the house and went back inside, stamping the snow off his boots. Susan was wrapping something in cheesecloth at the table, still wearing nothing but the sheet.

"I've put some of that cooked beef from last night in this," she said. "I've put some beans in this jar and some whiskey here. You got everything else you need in your saddlebags.''

He stuffed what she'd fixed in the pockets of his sheepskin, trying to avoid the sight of that shapely body so naked under the thin sheet. It was still cold in the room; her nipples were still erect under the cloth, and her breasts quivered heavily every time she moved.

She came to him now, standing near enough to touch, looking up into his eyes. "I wish you wouldn't go.''

He could feel the nearness of her stoking the fire inside him, the old lustful heat all mixed up with the anger any woman made him feel now. He searched for something to say, but whatever words he found got stuck in his throat.

She laid a hand on his chest, like maybe she knew that was as close as he would let her get. "What will I do if you don't come back?''

He looked away, itchy and uncomfortable at the pull he felt from her. Something about the closeness of her made him remember what Ganning had said, made him want to stay and not go after Foley at all. He closed that out of his mind. "I don't come back, you go ahead and do what you want to do. You got a place to spend the winter in if you want. You got my packhorse. I'm leaving the shotgun. You can use that to kill game. Probably be best to go to Price's. He and Ganning would take you in.''

She moved in against him then, so close he could feel her body softening against his, her head tucked just under his chin. He found his hand going around her waist, feeling the sleek curve of her back, uncomfortably aware of her breasts pillowing up against his chest. It was all he could do not to push her away.

"I'll be back," he said. "I ain't fixing to get killed. And you'll be all right. I asked Ganning to look in on you. Sit tight, and I'll see you in two or three days."

He was four miles along the road to Coffey before he remembered Coffey was where Bushnell's cook would be taking that wagon for supplies. He could have brought her with him. Put her on the packhorse and taken her to Coffey and put her on the train. Then he would have been rid of her. But it would mean turning back now, wasting time waiting for her to get her things together, maybe having to persuade her to leave. She could wait for Bushnell's wagon. He didn't want a woman on his hands. He wanted only one thing on his mind when he got to Coffey: how to kill Bob Foley.

# 13

It was noon of the next day when he reached Coffey.

He had bedded down in a snowsquall during the night, the wind whipping across those bleak plains like Ganning had said it would, but he couldn't sleep—it was too cold, and he couldn't get his mind to rest, burning as it was with thoughts of Foley, somewhere up ahead of him, Foley and what he had done and what it was he was running from.

He lay awake for what seemed like hours, drifting into dreams where he couldn't tell Susan from Anne and didn't know whether he could trust himself with either, coming awake drained and angry and eager to be moving again. He rose while it was still dark, ate some of the beef and beans Susan had fixed for him, and was on the road again by daybreak, riding head down, collar up against the wind, keeping the bay at an insistent and steady trot.

Toward noon the state of the road told him he was nearing town. Horses and wagons had passed along it already that morning, and the mud had turned the rutted snow to slush. The day was warming up, despite a thin overcast obscuring a pale and chilly sun. Sometime later Coffey itself came in sight, a good-sized collection of buildings sprawled out north and south along that flat prairie. Seeing it there quickened his blood, and he flicked the bay with his spurs.

He rode in along the urine-yellow streets, dodging freight wagons and buckboards and riders, surprised at how much traffic there was till he remembered it was a Saturday, market day. He saw no sign of Foley, but Foley would be holed up somewhere till that train was due to leave. He rode on till he found a stable, had his horse rubbed down and stalled, then sought a saloon where he could hole up himself till it was time to make his move.

At a quarter past two, itchy and impatient, he left the saloon and made his way along the crowded boardwalks till he found the train station on the eastern edge of town. The tracks passed along behind a last row of buildings there, and east beyond the tracks was just empty prairie. With a scarf up to shield his face, he paused on the boardwalk opposite the station while a mule team splashed past with a wagonload of crates. Then he crossed the slushy street and took a look in through the door.

Foley still hadn't showed. Probably aiming to wait till the last minute. He moved on up the boardwalk to lean against a corner building, where he could see along both streets. Then he rolled himself a smoke and waited.

By three o'clock he had smoked four cigarettes and was getting restless. The train was already in sight, a tiny black line on the horizon south of town, too far away to hear. By now the passing traffic had churned the slush to mud; for more than half an hour he had studied every rider splashing past, every man entering or leaving the station, and so far he'd seen nobody familiar. He was beginning to think Ganning was wrong about Foley when he saw Foley coming up the boardwalk toward him.

Foley was still a block from the station. He had sold his horse somewhere and was carrying his saddle on his shoulder. He wore a sheepskin coat open down the front to reveal his gunbelt and was walking with that loose and rangy gait Slocum recognized at once, the easy stride of a man without a care in the world. Slocum watched him tip his hat to two women, step down into the mud to let them pass, and then turn to watch the swing of their hips as they went on along the boardwalk, delicate hands holding their skirts up out of the mud. Foley said something after them. One of them flashed him a smile over her shoulder, and then Foley mounted the boardwalk again and came on, still wearing that charming grin he used on women.

Slocum knew what was on his mind. He remembered the times he'd spent with Foley and Beaumont and Quinn watching women pass along a boardwalk in one town or another, commenting on the rump of one and the bosom of another—laughing, judging which one would be good in bed—and he remembered now a bed in Jackson County, the bed he had shared with Anne, and felt a wave of heat sweep through his head and make his eyes go slitted like a cat's. In the pocket of his sheepskin, his hand closed around his spare Colt, a snub-nosed Shopkeeper's Model .45.

Foley drew even with the station and ducked inside. Slocum tucked the scarf up across his face and went in after him.

The station was one big high-ceilinged room, dim light falling through dirty windows front and back. Slocum put his back to the wall just inside the door. There were maybe a dozen people waiting for the train, all bundled up against the weather. The floor was greasy with mud, and the air was cold despite a stove glowing red in one corner. A pair of swinging doors led out onto the platform, and two long benches ran back-to-back across the center of the room. A third of the way down the far bench, his back to the door, was Bob Foley.

Slocum sidled around the end of the bench and eased down beside him. "Afternoon, Bob."

Foley flinched. For an instant he froze where he was, one hand reaching inside his coat for a sack of Bull Durham; then, carefully, he turned to meet Slocum's eyes, nothing but wariness showing on his face. For just one second he seemed about to say something; then he stifled whatever it was and bent to seize the saddle on the floor at his feet.

Slocum put his boot on the saddle and held it to the floor. "Stick around. I want to talk to you."

The boot had just grazed Foley's hand. Again he halted where he was, half bent over; then, carefully again, he eased back upright. A sidelong glance showed him the Colt Slocum had half out of his pocket. He laid his hands carefully on his thighs and subsided back against the bench.

"Thought you were back in the Hole. You get a sudden desire to catch a train?"

"No, I heard *you'd* got a sudden desire to catch a train. Didn't want you leaving without an old friend to see you off."

The train was coming into the station now, the engine, bristling with steam, moving like a black wall past that rear window, noise rolling through the station like a wave and drowning out all talk. Slocum heard it grind to a halt with a squeal of iron and a hiss of steam, and the passengers began milling out the doors

onto the platform. He could almost hear thought working behind Foley's eyes: Foley fixing where everybody was in the room, judging the distance to the
doors, trying without looking at him to decide whether
Slocum would shoot him cold if he made a dash for
the train.

"This is the last time we're ever going to see each
other," Slocum said. "Suppose we have a friendly
little talk. Suppose you tell me what happened back
there in Jackson County."

"You got some good reason why I should?"

Slocum felt that heat flare up behind his eyes. "You
tell me what happened, I'll kill you quick. Make me
work for it, and I'll find some way to make it last."

Foley had his composure back; he kept one eye on
the train, a trace of mockery in his smile. "Never
thought I'd see a woman do this to you. You sure you
didn't leave your balls back there in Jackson County?"

Cold air came in through the swinging doors.
Slocum watched Foley's eyes, seeing the little spark
of pleasure Foley was getting out of this. There had
always been that little spark between them—give and
take, challenge and response, each one trying to probe
the other, each one pleased to see the other couldn't
be made to back down. It had been the basis of what
had passed for friendship between them. Then he had
a flash of Foley struggling with Anne—and her naked
and desperate and screaming, likely feeling a kind of
fear he couldn't even imagine—and he felt that heat
beating through his brain again and the ice that followed it, hooding his eyes down and making his face
set like something left out too long in the cold.

That mocking smile returned to Foley's face, like
maybe he sensed he'd touched a nerve. "You losing

control, John? I hear you about went off half-cocked
there in Bushnell's. I tell you, living with that woman
down in Texas took something out of you."

"You ain't got much time to live. Better not waste
it talking bullshit. I want to know what happened with
Anne. I want to know which one of you put that knife
in her."

"I ain't got time to talk, John. I got a train to catch."

"You move, and I'll kill you where you sit."

The sounds of the train rose and fell as passengers
came through the doors, tracking more mud with them
as they came. Outside, the conductor was shouting
the call to board. From the engine came a loud scream
of the whistle, followed by the sharp *ding-ding-ding*
of the bell.

Foley was looking at him, pleased, mockingly de-
fiant. "You ain't going to kill me, John. Not cold like
this, where I can't defend myself."

Slocum leaned across to put his eyes close to Foley's, feeling the heat coming out of him in waves. "I
don't think you understand me. I didn't spend three
months tracking you from Texas to worry about the
rules when I found you. Thinking about killing you's
what's been keeping me alive. So don't count on any
ideas about what kind of man you think I am. Now
I want to know who killed Anne. And I want to hear
it fast and without any bullshit. You got maybe ten
seconds."

Foley lost his smile then and the spark in his eye.
"What makes you think I'd tell you if I knew?"

"You know. You were there. Who was it put the
knife in her?"

The passengers had boarded; the conductor was
hanging from a step-rail, swinging his lantern, shout-

ing the last call to board. The platform was crowded with recent arrivals and well-wishers waving goodbye to friends, and now the train began to move, huge blasts of sound hammering at the side of the station.

Foley was looking at him—probing him, judging him. "You won't shoot a man in the back." Abruptly he hoisted the saddle over his shoulder and headed for the doors out onto the platform.

Slocum was caught by surprise; by the time he pulled himself together and got to his feet, Foley was already out the doors. He pulled the Colt from his pocket and sprinted after him.

He collided with a woman carrying a satchel through the door, wrenched away from her, and burst outside. Foley was trotting awkwardly through the crowd, the saddle still slung over his shoulder. The train was sliding along the platform, picking up speed. The first two cars had cleared the end, and Foley was running for the step-rail at the front of the last car.

Slocum slipped on the muddy boards, righted himself, shoved a man out of the way, and dodged through the crowd. People began scattering out of his path; he hit another with his shoulder, cut around a baggage handler pulling his cart, and came clear of the crowd in time to see Foley swinging up the steps into the front of that last car. Slocum broke into a run and caught the last steps of the car and hauled himself up just as the caboose reached the end of the platform.

He hung there for a moment, getting his breath back, watching the crowd on the platform staring after him. Then he pulled himself up the steps and yanked the door open and slipped inside.

Foley had already passed through the far door into the next car. Slocum sprinted up the aisle, his Colt

out. Somebody shouted something, and a woman
screamed, but he ignored them, cleared the aisle, burst
through the far door, and crossed the rocking platform
in through the next. Foley was halfway up the aisle,
the saddle still over his shoulder.

"Foley?"

Foley turned. Surprise showed on his face; clearly
he hadn't expected Slocum to make the train. He
sighted the Colt in Slocum's hand, made as if to go
for his own, and then seemed to think better of it.
Indecision flickered across his face. Then he turned
to run on up the aisle, the saddle bouncing on his
shoulder.

Slocum shouted Foley's name and sprinted after
him again.

Now he saw shocked passengers rising from their
seats, startled faces turned his way—the round white
face of a woman in a bonnet, the wide eyes and open
mouth of a girl staring over a seat back. A man lunged
into the aisle and grabbed for his gun hand, but Slocum
stuck an elbow in the man's gut, shoved him aside,
and ran on. Foley had reached the far door. He fumbled with the latch, couldn't open it, kicked the door,
and turned to see Slocum still coming. He turned like
a man swinging an axe, slung the saddle through the
air, wrenched the door latch open, and burst on through.

The saddle hit Slocum in the face and ricocheted
into the seats, stirrups flailing. He found himself on
the floor, blood coming from his nose. A woman
screamed as the saddle hit her, and Slocum felt hands
reaching for him, somebody grappling with his gun
arm, somebody else hitting him on the ear. He came
up in a lunge, hit the first man he saw with all the
force he had in him, wrenched an arm loose, shoul-

dered another man out of the way, and leaped for the door. Then he was out onto the little rocking platform and through into the next car.

Foley was just going through the far door, reaching for the ladder leading up the back of the mail car. The train was picking up speed, the ground outside the windows streaming past. Slocum dodged the startled conductor, shoved another man back into his seat, and hit the door in mid-stride.

Foley was halfway up the ladder. Slocum leaped for him, got him by the back of the collar, and tried to pull him down. Foley kicked out behind him, both boots jerking in a sudden frenzy; Slocum felt a boot heel hit him in the gut and a wildly thrashing foot knock the .45 from his hand. He grabbed hold with both hands then and hauled Foley down off the ladder, the rocking of the car taking the platform suddenly out from under his feet so that both he and Foley landed on the metal floor, sliding.

Slocum grabbed for a handrail as his head went off the platform, the roadbed rushing past only a yard beneath him. Foley reared up and brought both clubbed fists down in a try for his face, but he rolled to the side, shook Foley off him, and came up on one knee. Another thrashing boot caught him in the chest; he tried to grab it, but Foley kicked him in the side with the other and wrenched around to seize a handrail with one hand, fumbling at his holster with the other.

Slocum rolled on his side, diving for his own holster. He was still on his back, bringing his Colt up, when Foley turned on his knees, firing at such close quarters that Slocum could feel the muzzle blast, could hear the slug whanging off the metal floor like an angry bee. He felt the Colt jump in his hand, and jump again, two shots so loud in between the cars he felt the sound of them hammering at his ears even above the rush of the train. Foley was hit in the belly, blown back against the ladder, where he hit like a sack of feed, slid to the floor, and lay there looking at Slocum with shocked and quizzical eyes, one arm hanging off the platform and swinging back and forth with the rocking of the car. Slocum watched the life drain out of his face till it was as dead as a doll's face and no longer anybody he even recognized.

He saw a man dart up in the window in the door of the car behind him, take one quick wide-eyed look, and dart down again. The women were still screaming. He holstered his Colt and got dizzily to his feet. The snow-covered ground was fleeing past on either side of the platform. Too fast, much too fast, but he had no choice. He moved to the edge of the platform, braced himself, and jumped.

He hit on his shoulder and rolled, careening wildly down the slope of the roadbed, legs flailing, the train rushing past just above him. He slammed into the ditch at the bottom of the roadbed, bounced, hit again, and rolled like a barrel, buffeting through clumps of sage, slamming and sliding and spinning. He grabbed for a sage clump, felt it ripped from his hands, and then he was sliding along the snow, turning and spinning, seeming to move faster on the slick snow cover, his boots digging deep gashes behind him as he tried to stop himself. And then he hit something else, some hump in the ground that sent him into the air again, and this time when he landed he hit so hard he lost his senses for an instant. It was only when he got them back that he realized he had stopped and was lying still.

He stayed on his back while his head cleared, afraid to move. The train had gone; he could hear the sound of it fading. His heartbeat pulsed in his ears. After a while, he became aware of the snow, wet and cold beneath him. He took a long, slow breath, and felt no pain. No ribs were broken. Then, gingerly, he moved a leg, then an arm, testing for pain. He eased a shoulder up, rose to an elbow. When he was sure his back was all right, he eased over onto his side, pulled his legs up, and got to his knees.

A wave of dizziness went through him. He shook his head, blinking against the weak sunlight reflecting off the snow. When the dizziness passed, he rose to his feet and stood painfully erect, feeling his spine pop. He hurt all over, and the back side of him was wet through where he had slid along the snow, but he was whole. The train was receding into the distance, a tiny dot on the immense expanse of prairie. He saw his Colt in the snow a few yards up the tracks, and his hat lying at the base of the roadbed. Carefully, limping a little, he retraced the path of his long slide, holstered the Colt, retrieved his hat, and turned back the way he had come.

The town was a good two miles back. The tracks stretched away in a straight line toward the little station, where he could see tiny figures still standing on the platform. Wearily, he put his hat on and started back along the tracks toward town.

# 14

He reached Hobbs' Hole and the shack after dark the next evening. He had spent the night in between in a bare hotel room in Coffey, wanting to give his bruised and battered body a rest. He had drunk himself to sleep to keep from thinking and woke at dawn hung over and dry-mouthed and left town as soon as he could stomach food. The hangover had dulled his mind, but that was good. A long ride could put a man's thoughts to working on things better left alone, and Slocum didn't want to think.

It snowed the whole way back, a steady, driving storm that was hard to see through. The snow from the day before had mostly melted off, but the ground had frozen again during the night, and he could tell this was going to last. The drifts were three feet high by the time he reached the Hole. The bay snorted and broke into a trot when he turned it off the road, sensing it was almost home. He was out of the wind now, and the snow slacked off. Halfway up through the trees he saw lamplight seeping through the windows of the shack, promising warmth and company inside, and he kicked the bay on into a lope. Seeing those lights made him feel a whole hell of a lot better than he liked to admit.

He took his time unsaddling and seeing to the horse. Susan would have heard him dismount at the back of the shack, and knowing what he'd gone to Coffey for, she would be wondering what to expect. He wasn't sure what to expect himself.

She was curled on the bed reading a penny dreadful from her pack when he stepped inside, carrying his gear. He stowed the saddle in the corner behind the door, tossed his hat and coat after it, and watched her lay the book down and rise from the bed. She was wearing an outfit he hadn't seen before, her breasts bulging out a white shirtwaist above a coarse pleated skirt, like maybe she had dressed for the occasion, but now that he was here she seemed unsure of herself, not meeting his eyes. Finally she said, "I kept some supper warm for you, in case you got back tonight," and padded in her bare feet to the hearth to spoon up meat and beans onto a tin plate.

She retreated to her book on the bed while he ate, returning only to take the plate and utensils when he'd finished. He hadn't planned on doing any drinking, but he didn't fancy sitting idle by himself. Some talk would be welcome, but she was curled up on the bed again, her feet tucked under her, not looking up from her book, as if afraid of the mood he was in. He uncorked the bottle and splashed some whiskey into his glass.

The picture on the wall drew his eyes to it like a magnet. The ragged edge showed where he'd torn off the strip with Charley on it, leaving Foley and Quinn and himself, and he could see Foley clear, but knowing Foley was dead now did nothing to relieve that gnawing in his gut. He put his mind on Coffey, trying to work up some satisfaction at what had happened there, remembering the cool and self-assured way Foley had hoisted that saddle and left the station, so sure he wouldn't get shot in the back; the look on his face the first time he'd turned in the train, having been so sure he'd got away alive; the last look on his face as he lay on that rocking mail car platform, realizing finally that he hadn't.

That didn't help, either. Foley was dead, but something about it was left undone, as if killing Foley wasn't enough and he had to go on now and hunt down Foley's ghost and kill that, too, and keep on hunting ghosts till there weren't any left to kill. For a moment, everything he'd done since leaving Texas seemed like wasted effort, and he had a sudden fear he was going to carry that gnawing around in his gut from here on out, like some little predatory animal in there, eating away at him till he died.

In this way he drank a good quarter of what was left in the bottle, brooding at the picture on the wall. He wasn't drunk; wasn't anywhere near drunk. He was cold sober and he seemed to be getting more so with every drink, and by now he knew he could drink the bottle dry and still be as sober as he was when he started. The only sound in the room was the crackle of the fire in the fireplace, the chink of the bottle against the glass as he poured another drink, the little whisper of Susan turning a page of her book. Her silence was beginning to get to him. He had expected questions, some need to know what had happened in Coffey, and only now that she wasn't asking did he realize the need he had to tell it to her.

He heard the creak of the bed slats now as she got to her feet. She came to take the chair at the other end of the table, scooting up so she could prop her elbows in front of her. Now she started picking at her nails, trying to meet his eyes and not succeeding very well.

"You trying to get drunk?" she said.

He gave her a mock salute with the glass. "I doubt that's possible."

He watched her breasts swell against the fabric of her shirtwaist. She saw where his eyes were, and a flush rose up her face, and he could see her trying to call up something to say, something likely sharp and cutting. Whatever it was, she shut it off and closed her mouth on it. He watched her eyes glance from his face to the mirror and back again, and then she rose from her chair and brought the picture from the mirror and threw it on the table in front of him.

"That's what you been looking at all night. You might as well go ahead. Go ahead and burn it. I know what happened in Coffey. I could tell soon as you walked in the door."

He looked at the picture. A ragged edge where Charley Beaumont had been. Bob Foley, dead now on that train out of Coffey. And Paul Quinn and himself. It was just a picture.

"You want me to do it for you?" she said. "Would that make you feel better?"

He didn't answer.

"Which one was it?" She held the picture up so she could get a look at it. "Are you taking them in line? Is that the way you're doing it? First the one on the left and then the next one and the next one?" She laid a finger on Bob Foley's chest. "Is that the one? Is he the one you killed today?"

"Yesterday."

"Is he the one? Is he the one that's dead now?"

"He's the one."

With a twist of her wrist she tore Foley's picture from the rest and crossed to the hearth and threw it in the fire.

He sprang after her and caught her arm, but the picture was already burning. The last thing he saw was Foley's grin shrinking into instant flame.

She had recoiled half away from him, eyes wary as a cat's, her arm suddenly strong as steel as she tried to pull it from his grasp. He reached for her other wrist, but she thrust it behind her and stood there trembling, head half-turned away, watching him.

"There was no need for that," he said.

"You killed him, didn't you? You'd have stared at it half the night if I hadn't."

"It's nothing to do with you."

"It is to do with me." Her breasts swelled that shirtwaist every time she breathed. "I have to live with it. Can't you talk to me? Even if it's just to kill somebody, you got a reason to be here. I've got nothing. I can't stand this being alone. Even when you're here I'm alone."

Struck by the plea in her voice, he laid a hand alongside her neck, felt the warmth of her skin and the beat of her blood, and then that edginess came back and he pulled the hand away and held it out away from him like something soiled, but she reached for it and seized it and pulled it back to where he'd had it, brought her other arm up, too, and with it the hand gripping her wrist, and pressed that hand against her throat.

"You can. I'm making no claims on you. That wagon's going out in a week. I'll be on it if you want. But, my good God, can't we just be together? Take what there is without all this walking on eggs we do around each other?"

The plea was in her eyes as well as her voice. Before he could think about it, he had closed his hands around the nape of her neck and pulled her to him.

Her hands came up around his own neck. Her mouth reached for his hot and hungry. She molded herself to him then, her breasts swelling against his chest, and for the first time in months he could feel. Could feel the smooth silkiness of her skin under his hands, the wet warmth of her mouth, the soft pressure of her tongue as her head dipped and turned, her lips retreating and returning to seek his again.

He knew she had been a stranger to him till now, but now all restraint had vanished. Heat and hardness rose at his groin, and he slid a hand down to pull her in against him there, and now her head sank back in the cup of his other hand and her eyes came slowly open—soft, defenseless, welcoming. He picked her up and carried her to the bed and began stripping off her clothes.

Naked, he sank in against her, inside her, marvelling at the touch of those big breasts against his chest, every inch of his skin so alive to the feel of her that he felt he had been dead all these past months and was only now coming back to life. She had his face in her hands, holding his head in place while her mouth fed off his. He couldn't get enough of the feel of her; even as he moved in her he stroked the supple curves and slopes of her body, feeling her respond to his touch, her belly arching in toward his, the huge globes of her breasts moving and shifting heavily against him, her eyes going closed every now and then as the small sounds began to come from her throat, and then the eyes opening again to gaze at him with that soft and defenseless welcome.

For what seemed an hour they writhed together, one mouth feeding off the other, hands roaming flesh, bodies rocking in that slow, sweet pleasure till the feeling began to build inside and the slowness no longer sufficed and they climbed through heated cries into a rhythmic dance so fierce he no longer knew what was him and what her, climbing till they reached some delirious plateau where no thought existed or could exist, where there was nothing but touch and taste, sounds and sighs and endless movement; then slowing again, moving close, descending slowly to a place where he was aware of himself again, and aware of her, so that they could begin that fiercely passionate climb all over again.

When it was over, she lay cuddled in his arms for a very long time. He had no need for thought, no wish to move. Finally she let her head sink back in the crook of his arm, eyes shining up at him.

"That's what we needed," she murmured. "Not that angry other thing."

He touched a hand to her face and dipped his mouth to hers. "It wasn't you I was mad at."

"I know. But it's better this way. I couldn't have taken the other anymore."

"Don't think about it," he said. "Don't think about anything."

And he felt himself begin to rise and harden again, felt her shift and move to give him entry again; he sank deep inside her and just stayed there, content to be in her, close together, skin to skin.

# 15

It snowed all that night and all the next day, a steady snowfall blown damned near sideways by a driving wind, and by evening of the second day he knew they were in for a blizzard. He took the hand axe up into the orchard then and cut what he figured would be enough firewood to last them through and stacked it around the walls inside the shack. He stabled the horses in the old woodshed out back, where he could see to them without having to fight the wind, and set about chinking what cracks remained around the doors. By dark he figured the shack was snug enough to last out any blizzard.

Susan had been busy at the hearth while he worked. He could admit now how good it was to have her there, to have a woman moving quietly and purposefully around the house, how good it was to see her sitting across from the table from him while he ate, how good it was to slide into bed and find her already waiting there, already naked, already reaching for him, warm and willing and eager, and how good it was to lose himself in that mindless lunging rhythm that seemed to drown even the howl of the storm outside.

This time when it was over she lay a long time cuddled up against him. Above the snap and pop of the coals in the fire he could hear her steady breathing. Every now and then a sudden burst of wind would beat against the skins over the windows or the horses would move restlessly in the woodshed against the back wall. After a while she pulled away from him and lay on her back; he could tell she was chewing over something in her mind.

"It's blowing very hard," she said finally.

"We're all right. We got rations and firewood aplenty. We can ride it out."

She was silent for a long while again. Then: "How long do you think it will last?"

"Can't tell. Two days. A week. Winters get bad in this country."

He figured she was thinking about that supply wagon Bushnell was due to send out to Coffey. Likely Bushnell had a sledge he could harness a team to for winter travel, but if this blizzard kept up long enough even a sledge might not make it out. Hobbs' Hole could be snowed in for as long as a month. He wondered if she was still counting on something like that. A woman who set her mind on a thing could make herself believe it was going to happen no matter what the odds looked to be, and she was as stubborn as any woman he could call to mind. But thinking those thoughts stirred up the old edginess inside him, and he didn't want that. To keep from thinking, he rolled over toward her and slid a hand up the warm slope of her belly. She moved in against him with a welcome little murmur, one sleek thigh sliding up across his hip, and the feel of her breasts swelling against his chest started bringing him up again. She was a good remedy for thinking.

The blizzard kept up for a week. Every morning when he woke he listened for the silence that would mean it had stopped, and every morning he would hear again the howl of the wind up under the eaves, and when he crept from the bed to peer out a window, the snow would be blowing so hard he could barely see the outhouse in the orchard and he would know they were in for another day of it. He would return to bed then, wake Susan from the warmth of sleep and start again the one thing that could take him out of himself, that mindless oblivion they made together, but not even that could go on forever, and he would have to face the day then and the thoughts in his mind again.

The waiting was almost more than he could stand. He had finished the whiskey the day after he'd returned from Coffey, so there was not even the sop of drink to dull his mind with, and he couldn't get himself to concentrate enough to read that penny dreadful Susan had been carrying around in her pack. He had broken down each of his firearms and cleaned and oiled the actions till they worked finer and smoother than they had the day he'd bought them. He got out his saddle soap then and worked over his gunbelt and his boots and every piece of leather he owned, till even the saddle soap was gone and there was nothing left to do but wait and think and remember.

Occasionally his restlessness would get to him, and he would pace the shack till the walls seemed to start closing in. He would go out to check the horses then, or to bring in water from the rain barrel, or to cut and split and add to the stacks around the walls firewood they didn't even need. Twice, unable to stand it anymore, he bundled up and took the Winchester and spent half the day looking for deer in the timber above the orchard, following likely-looking trails head down against the wind, holing up in some sheltered pocket near what he figured was a likely bedding ground, relishing the cold and glad to be out, though he saw only one deer and that too late and too far away to get a shot. That was all right. It wasn't the kill he needed but the hunt. Anything to get him out of the shack, where he could not escape his thoughts—the memory of that bloody kitchen floor in Texas, or Charley Beaumont rotting in a shallow grave out there beside the road, or Bob Foley carrying a saddle up a slushy boardwalk toward a cold and dirty train station, still wearing the last smile he would ever use to charm a woman.

Out in the woods during the day he could get away from thoughts like that, but nightfall trapped him indoors. He would try to avoid the mirror on the wall then, with its torn and faded picture. He would pace the shack, restless and uneasy, every now and then peeling the deerhide away from a window to see if the blizzard showed any signs of blowing itself out, trying without success not to think of Quinn and Walker in that house up in Hobbs' Pocket, likely watching the snow same as he was, wondering when the storm would stop, wondering what was coming when it did.

Always then Susan would come to lock her hands across the flat of his belly, her breasts swelling softly against his back, her warm body pressed up against his. "Don't," she would say. "Don't think about them. Don't think about anything. Just hold me. Hold me and don't think."

And the feel of her would bring him around, around to meet her warm wet mouth and her softened eyes; his hands would be on her before he knew it, loosing the buttons to bare that ripe and shapely body, and soon they would be on the bed again, lost in that lovely writh-

ing rocking dance that was the only thing he knew that
could blot the thoughts and memories from his mind.
In bed with her, he could forget Hobbs' Hole existed,
or Hobbs' Pocket, or that there was anybody anywhere
but in this bed, in this one warm room.

"This is all there is," she said once afterward, lying
warm and sated in the hollow of his arm. "Just this
one minute. I read that somewhere." She was idly
stroking the hair on his chest, her soft eyes on his
face. "Sometimes I work at believing that. When I
can make it work, everything's different. I feel things
so much stronger. Like when you're inside me, and
we're doing what we do. It takes me over then. It's
all I am. Or standing with the door open sometimes
when you're out hunting and watching to see if I can
find you coming back. I do it then, work hard at
making myself believe this one minute is all there is,
and when I can do it, the whole of God's outdoors is
like . . . it's like I don't really see it other times. How
beautiful it is."

He had a sense of what she meant. Often just before
or after a fight the world would come alive like that—
after a battle during the War sometimes, when they'd
put the blue-bellies to a run, or sometimes actually
during a battle, the way the fighting went, like the
flow of a river, till sometimes you could almost say
there was beauty in the battle itself. He remembered
once riding at the head of a column of cavalry along
a narrow dirt road through a stand of live oak on a
warm afternoon and hearing off in the brush the scuffle
of hooves and clank of equipment that was a company
of Yankee cavalry moving unawares toward them and
the sweet, swift rush of his blood as quietly there
under the shadowy ceiling of trees he had turned his

men right flank and led them carefully off the road into the deeper gloom of the woods till he saw the first faint blur of the bluebellies approaching, and the sudden thrill in his throat when he'd loosed a Rebel yell and led that wild reckless yelping charge through the summery afternoon that routed Yankees into pell-mell flight and spilled them from their saddles and left them strewn among the trees like so many blue-clad scarecrows blown down by a sudden storm.

That was one time the whole green and glistening afternoon had been alive to him in the way she meant it—vivid and real, till the very trees seemed to quiver in the light. That memory never failed to bring back to him how alive he had felt in the War. Other people could say killing was wrong, but they didn't know what he knew. Sometimes there could be beauty in a battle. That was what made wars what they were, what made men like himself who couldn't seem to stop needing a fight even when the wars were over.

He liked her for stirring that memory up in him, for talking the way she had. In other circumstances, he figured he might have learned to like her even more. She had spunk, the kind of courage that kept a woman alive in country like this. And there was always her astonishing body and the pleasure she knew how to give in bed—and the pleasure she knew how to get. The best kind of woman in bed was the kind who could feel as much pleasure as she gave. Occasionally then, later, pacing the floor or peering out at the driving snow, he would think about it, about maybe sticking with her, telling her to forget that supply wagon Bushnell would be sending out—do like Ganning had suggested and take her with him when this was over and try to work again into the kind of thing he had had with Anne. But as soon as he had the thought, the old edginess would return, growing rapidly into the fuming anger he had no control over and didn't understand, and he knew it would never work. If he tried it, he would only end up driving her away from him. Better to let it go.

He would put his mind back where it ought to be then; he would lie awake in the night thinking with the old heat seething in his brain of Frank Walker and Paul Quinn up there snug in Hobbs' Pocket, thinking of what he would do when the blizzard stopped, thinking that when he had flushed them out and learned which of them had knifed the one woman he'd wanted enough to stick with—and killed the both of them just to make sure—then he would be able to breathe again without this feeling he was fanning flames in a furnace somewhere down inside.

He would catch fleeting memories then of Quinn, glimpses of his grin in some border-town saloon when they were younger and having a night on the town, cocksure and still young enough to think they were going to live forever, discussing the women in the place and haggling over which one to try, drinking themselves into that fine high place where a man knew he was living better than anybody ever had, whooping and fighting and laughing, and riding out some nights drunk on horseback and shooting out streetlamps for the whole length of a cowtown street.

You never knew where life was going to take you. Nobody ever told you it might bring you to a place where the one thing you needed to keep you sane was to kill the men you'd thought were the best friends you ever had.

# 16

The day before Bushnell's supply wagon was due to go out, the blizzard finally let up.

He woke that morning to a silence so unexpected it rang in his ears like a bell. The fire was still putting out heat. The room was so warm it was almost stifling. Susan had kicked the bear robe down during the night and was lying asleep on her belly, one knee drawn up, one large breast bulging out beneath the cradle of her arm. For a moment he watched the curve of her breast swell with her breathing, curbing an urge to run his hand down the slope of her back. He eased out of bed so as not to wake her and pulled his pants on. Then he crossed the board floor to the window, removed the chinking, and tugged the deerhide back away from the jamb.

The snow had stopped. The wind had died to a dead calm. The sky was still overcast, but it was thinning overhead; he could see a weak sun trying to burn its way through. Likely it would clear off by noon. The drifts were deep down the slope of the hill, but a man could move if he had to.

He turned to see that Susan was awake. She was up on one elbow, watching him, one arm cradled across her breasts. He was struck by how good it was to look at her, naked and voluptuous, so at ease with him now it didn't occur to her to pull the bear robe up.

"The blizzard's stopped," she said.

"Stopped during the night sometime. The sun's coming out."

"Is it . . . Do you think you'll be going, then?"

"Be going to Price's soon as I've grained the horses. I want to talk to Ganning. Likely I can hit that bunch in Hobbs' Pocket tomorrow."

She seemed to think on that for a moment, but if she had anything to say about it, she kept it to herself. She swung to the edge of the bed, still cradling her breasts while she fished for her clothes with her other hand. "I'd best fix you some breakfast then," she said. "You can't ride that far hungry."

The sky was clear and the sun out by the time he left for Price's place. The snow had drifted stirrup-high in places, and he had to use the spurs to break the bay through some of it, but it felt good to be out of the shack, out in air so cold he had a sense one good loud noise would put a crack in the sky. Susan hadn't said anything more about his leaving; likely she knew making a fuss would do her no good, but he figured she would try to change his mind when the time came. He would deal with that when he had to.

He stuck to the hills along the eastern rim of the Hole, avoiding Bushnell's, and came down on Price's place through the timber up back of the clearing. Smoke was pouring from the cabin chimney, and he saw that Price had a stove going in the chicken house to keep his hens from freezing. He rode on in, setting the dog to barking in the barn, and reined up back of the cabin. He was knocking snow from his boots when he heard the door open and saw Ganning standing there waiting for him.

"Bit restless, ain't you?" Ganning said. "Snow's

barely stopped, and here you are out in it. Come on in where it's warm."

Inside, Slocum shucked his sheepskin and went to stand by the fire. Price sat on a stool beside the hearth, stripping corn for his chickens, the dried kernels clattering into a tin pail between his knees.

"See you weathered through," he said. "How'd that shack stand the blizzard?"

"We survived, but I don't aim to sit another one out." Slocum accepted a cheroot from Ganning and fished a burning stick from the fire to light it with. "Another good storm like that, and I might get snowed in for the winter."

"Be a good thing if you did," Price said. "Maybe by then you'd get over that foolishness you came here for. You still thinking on that?"

"I had a bellyful of thinking this past week. Thinking will drive a man mad if he don't do something about it. I aim to go hit that bunch at Hobbs' place tomorrow."

Ganning shook his head. "You better give it some more thought. Getting cabin-bound in a storm makes a man edgy. You get restless, then you get reckless. I know the feeling. You'll do something foolish just to break out of it. Wait on it a while, and you'll see I'm right."

"I'm through waiting. I'd feel better with somebody backing me up, but I aim to do it, with help or without."

"You'll just get yourself killed. There's no way even the three of us could pull it off."

"The two of you," Price said. "Leave me out of this. It's foolhardy, the whole idea, and I won't be a part of it."

"I know you're dead set against it," Slocum said, "but I got me a plan worked out. If things break right, I think it'll work."

"Don't matter what plan you got," Ganning said. "The fact you even got a plan shows how your mind's addled. No plan ever made could get them two out of that place—less'n you had as many men as Hobbs has got. And you ain't."

Slocum took a last drag on the cheroot and threw it in the fire. "Well, I didn't figure you'd go along. Just thought I'd ask." He shouldered back into his sheepskin and settled his hat on his head. "What I really came for was on account of Susan. Bushnell's supposed to send his cook out to Coffey for supplies tomorrow. I told Susan to catch a ride with him. I ain't sure she will. I'd appreciate your riding over to see if she's gone. If she's not, look after her for me."

Price finished taking the kernels off a cob and tossed the cob into the fire. "Bushnell may not send out for supplies tomorrow. Could be he'll wait till the weather's better. Maybe you ought to tell her different. Take a closer look at what it is you're giving up. A man ought to count himself lucky she wants to tie up with him."

"She put those ideas in your head?"

"She never mentioned it. I could just see that's what she favored. I got the idea she liked having you around."

"Well, I want her on the road to Coffey. She can catch a train out of there to wherever it is she wants to go. She's better off without me." To Ganning, he said, "I'm obliged for your help. Sorry you can't see your way clear to helping further, but I'll handle it on my own."

"Every man picks his own way to die," Ganning

said. "You're set on it. You do it."

Slocum had put Ganning and Price out of his mind by the time he got back to the shack—them, and everything they had said. He wasn't planning on dying any time soon, and he wasn't going to change his mind about Susan. If she was planning to try to change it for him, she gave no sign of it. From the way she acted, a man could believe this was a day no different from any other. She spent the afternoon heating water in the iron pot and scrubbing what clothes needed washing, and after supper, while he readied his gear at the table, she dug a sewing kit out of her pack and went to mending the hem of a dress, curled up on the bed as usual.

He had everything ready but the shotgun and he was working on it now. He had unfastened the sling from the metal ring in the butt and pulled it out through the ring at the other end, just under the twin muzzles. Now he was braiding himself a thin little cord out of strips of deerhide, anchoring one end of it to that ring under the muzzles and working the rest into a yard-wide noose with a slip knot he could snug up tight. He had it fixed the way he wanted it and was propping the shotgun in the corner by the door when he heard the bed creak as Susan got to her feet.

"You want me to fix you something to eat?" she said. "Something to carry with you tomorrow? There's some meat left. And I can put some beans in a jar."

He watched her take in the sight of the noose hanging from the Greener, but if she had any questions about it, she didn't ask them. He brought the bay's bridle over by the fire so the bit would be warm when he saddled up in the morning, and sat down at the table to pull his boots off.

"Just fix me some meat. Some meat and maybe a

little bread. I don't want to be carrying anything bulky."

She kept herself busy fixing his rations while he stripped down and got in under the bear robe. Then she turned down the lamp till the wick guttered out and came to undress beside the bed, with only the red light flickering from the fire still to see by.

She stepped out of her skirt and stripped off the rest of what she had on, and then she just stood there, hugging herself, looking at him. He figured she was giving him a special look to remind him of what he was giving up, but he didn't care what her reasons were—she was something to look at. The firelight struck a line up the curve of her legs, shadowing the gentle slope of her belly, leaving the little triangle dark between her thighs. Without her bulky clothes she always looked surprisingly small, with a delicate waist and a body so slim it made those astonishingly large breasts look even bigger than they were. He always felt a little awkward because he couldn't take his eyes off her breasts.

"Will you be leaving early tomorrow?" she said.

"Leaving before dawn. I'll be gone before you're awake."

She brought her hands down to her sides then, standing there naked and exposed, as if to present herself to him. "Do you want me? Or do you need to sleep?"

"I'll worry about sleep later. Come here." And he slung open the bear robe and the blankets, reaching for her as she crept onto the bed.

She seemed out of control as soon as he was in her. Her body arched up like a tautened spring, already shuddering, deep animal sounds already coming from her throat. She was wilder than he'd ever known her to be, and for an instant he thought she was faking it, trying to bind him to her, but then he knew she wasn't. Some desperate need was working in her, some lonely hunger that came from a long way back, likely stirred up now by knowing he would be gone in the morning, leaving her alone again—alone again like she'd been when that man of hers, Jesse, had got himself killed in the spring—with nothing to look forward to now but a long cold ride across ninety miles of winter prairie to a strange town out in the middle of nowhere and a lonely train ride to God knew where after that, to try to start over again a life that didn't look to have been too good to her so far. He could feel all that working itself out in her, putting real hunger in the mouth she lifted to feed off his, putting real heat in the way she drove her body again and again against his so that they became together one mindlessly ceaseless movement that went on for a very long time, belly sliding against belly, skin against skin, the room filled with those small and secret sounds a woman made only in bed with a man, and as he felt surging up within him a heat that he could tell would take him far out beyond control himself he heard a strange and strangled cry wrenched from deep inside her, a cry that stammered and stumbled and sorted itself into words—a wish, a hope, a wistfully desperate plea.

"There's just this," she cried. "Ain't it so? There's just this minute. There's nothing else. There's nothing else but us here now...."

And, gripping her face in his hands, his hips lunging, feeling oblivion rising like black floodwater into his brain, he poured his hot breath into her ear: "Yes, yes, there's just us here, this now—there's nothing

else, and never has been and never will be and never
could be," and he knew by the way she broke that the
words had sent her over.

She cried out some incoherent word, arched up
shuddering in his arms, bucked and buckled and shud-
dered up again and collapsed in against him, shaking
like she was holding in tears. "It could be!" she cried.
"We could make it be. We could stay the winter here.
They'd winter in, or they'd leave, but you wouldn't
have to go. This don't have to change."

That black oblivion rose up uncontrollably in him,
climbing the back of his neck till it flooded into his
brain and only his body moved on, thrusting and lunging like some animal mortally wounded but unable to
die, his hands holding her in a death grip of their own,
his breath rushing hot in her ear till he too buckled
and broke and collapsed down against her, shaking
too with whatever it was that got loose in him when
being with a woman put him out of control.

He felt himself begin to go immediately cold. Before he could stop himself, he pulled away, withdrew
from her, and lay on his back at the side of the bed,
feeling that black death slowly draining out of him,
aware once again of where he was and what morning
would bring, unable even knowing it was coming to
keep the coldness out of his voice.

"I don't want to hear that talk again," he said.
"Now the snow's stopped, they could be heading out,
and I'd never know it. And Bushnell's cook's going
out to Coffey tomorrow. We ain't talked about that
in a while, but you know he's going. We agreed you'd
go with him when he did. Ain't nothing happened to
change that."

She had turned away and was facing the wall, her

back to him. The coals popped and snapped in the
fire, but her silence was the loudest thing in the room.
He wanted to reach for her, tell her what he knew to
be true—that she was better off without him, that
something in her called to something brutal in himself,
and if they stuck together they would only kill whatever it was each was looking for in the other—but
he knew it would do no good. It wouldn't help her,
even if she could hear the truth in what he said.

The game always ended this way. Sooner or later
she had to call in the cards. And when she did, it
turned out she'd had that hole card all along. The one
that said she wanted to make this permanent; that no
matter what rules she'd laid down when you agreed
to play, she wanted you to stay and not move on.
Secretly, she believed her hole card was wild, and it
took a world of hurt before she learned there were no
wild cards in the game. He always knew he should
buy out before the game even started; every time he
didn't he got in so deep it was like cutting flesh to
get out again. Losing Anne had cut so deep it had
taken not only his heart and his soul but his entrails
as well. He didn't plan on getting in that deep again.

"I'll leave you the packhorse," he said. "You can
ride it to the road and tie it on behind and sell it in
Coffey. That'll give you the price of a ticket and
something to live on for a while."

She didn't say another word. After a while he
reached for the box of cheroots he kept under the bed
and lit one and lay on his back watching the smoke
disappear in the firelight. All that long while, she
stayed the way she was, her back to him, so still he
could barely hear her breathing. When he'd smoked
the cheroot down till it burned his fingers, he flicked

it into the fireplace and rolled on his side, facing the wall same as she was, settling down for sleep.

She turned then and crept up against him, molded her warm body against his, breasts swelling against his chest, her head tucked down under his chin. She didn't look at him, and she didn't say anything, and though he'd just told her he would be gone before she woke in the morning, she didn't try to get him to talk anymore, not even to say goodbye.

# 17

Daybreak found him lying in the hay at the edge of
the loft in Hobbs' barn. He had been there an hour,
waiting, listening, hearing only the rustle of mice, the
flutter of a bat up under the rafters, the stirring of the
bull in a stall down below.

He had located the bull earlier, after making his
way on foot across the snow-covered Pocket to the
barn. Moving by feel in the dark, he had found three
horses in separate stalls and the bull in another stall
midway along the aisle. He was relieved to find the
horses. He had left his own up on the ridge to the
west because there was no place to hide it down here
and he had been planning to jump one out of the corral.
He threw saddle and bridle on a roan in the stall nearest
the rear door and climbed up into the loft, to where
he would be able to watch the bull.

It was cold in the loft. He had lain awake in the
dark, uncomfortably aware of Walker and Quinn in
the house only yards away. To avoid thinking about
them he thought of Susan, remembering rising from
the bed in the dark and the sight of her asleep in the
glow of the hearth, lying on her belly, the blankets
kicked down around her ankles, one knee drawn up
and that voluptuous body bared to his gaze; and then
remembering her began to make him uncomfortable,
too, and he tucked his hands up under his arms and

just blanked out his mind till the first faint flush of dawn came seeping through the cracks around the doors.

He had to wait another twenty minutes for Hobbs, and by then it was light enough to see. He checked the horse, hoping the sides of the stall would keep Hobbs from seeing it was rigged for riding. Below him he could see the bull, a blooded English Durham—Hobbs' pride, the bait that was going to bring Hobbs under the gun. He had his gloves off and was trying to rub his hands warm when the tall doors creaked at the front of the barn and he heard Hobbs slip inside. Quietly, he tucked the gloves in his pocket, put his head down in the hay, and lay still.

The doors creaked closed, and he heard the faint sounds of Hobbs crossing the earthen floor to where the bull was stalled. For a short while all sounds ceased. Then he heard the low murmur of Hobbs' voice, coming from the direction of the stall. When he had figured out what it was, he raised his head and peered down over the hay.

Hobbs was leaning over the stall door, his back to the loft, the position he was in hiking his sheepskin up just enough to show a holster strapped to one thigh. He was murmuring something to the bull and rubbing at the spot between its horns.

Slocum couldn't make out the words. He listened off behind him to make sure nobody else was coming along the path. Then, slowly, making as little noise as possible, he rose to his knees and levelled the shotgun at Hobbs' back.

"Hold it where you are, Hobbs. I got a ten-gauge shotgun pointing right at your back."

The first sound brought Hobbs halfway up out of

the stall. Now he went stiff where he was, hands propped on the stall door, one leg canted awkwardly out where he'd been about to swing around. His head was bowed, almost like a man praying, and he was listening hard as any man ever had.

Slocum rose to his feet and eased sideways toward the head of the ladder. "You made a mistake, Hobbs. You let 'em hide out up here. That brings you in on it."

Trying not to turn around looked to be costing Hobbs effort. Finally, he said, "I know that voice. Even hearing it one time, I know that voice. I warned you once, Slocum, but it's clear you're not in your right mind. You're like a mad dog, and a mad dog's got to be shot out of simple decency."

"You wouldn't be the first to try," Slocum said, "nor the first that died trying."

The bull stirred in its stall, knocking a horn up against a stanchion. Slocum reached the ladder, grasped an upright with his free hand, and lowered one foot till he found a rung. Then he started down, hanging off the ladder by one hand so he could keep the Greener on Hobbs' back. He could almost see the way Hobbs was straining to hear where he was.

"You've put your head in a noose now," Hobbs said. "This won't work. There's a good dozen men here you'll have to deal with. You can't kill a dozen men."

"You only got to worry about me killing one. You keep yourself alive, and I'll handle the others." Slocum was on the ground now, listening for any sounds from the buildings around the house. His breath plumed white in the still air of the barn. He worked the knot of the noose he'd fashioned the night before, so that the noose hung free from the ring on the Greener's barrel. "I'm going to come up behind you now. Stay easy, and you'll stay alive."

Hobbs looked to be fighting the urge to bolt. A cold sweat had started breaking out on his face. "I'll give you Quinn," he said. "You can have Quinn, but I can't give you Walker. He's kin, Slocum. You're from the South, they tell me; you know I can't give up kin. You take Quinn and leave Walker to me. If I find he had a hand in that Texas business, I'll take him to the law myself."

"You already know he had a hand in it. That's why he's on the run. And I don't want the law to get him. *I* want him."

Close behind Hobbs now, he eased the Greener's barrels up under the man's jaw, just forward of his ear, and slipped the noose over his head. "See, it wasn't my head I was fixing to put in a noose." He cinched it tight, snugging the shotgun muzzle up under Hobbs' chin. "Careful now, Hobbs. I'm going to unbutton your coat and get that gunbelt off you. The littlest thing goes wrong, this shotgun's going to blow your brains all over the wall. You want to make sure that don't happen. You think you can be that careful?"

"For God's sake, man, don't be a fool." Hobbs stood stiff as a stake, his head canted awkwardly up and to one side, his neck so rigid it seemed suddenly frozen to his spine. He had to swallow hard to get more words out. "You can't do this. That's icy ground out there. One slip and you'll kill me."

"That's the idea."

"I mean a slip. Not even trying to kill me. You need me. You kill me, they'll fall on you like wolves, Slocum. They'll shoot you to pieces before you can move."

"I ain't aiming to slip. You better make sure you don't."

Holding the shotgun carefully in place with one hand, he leaned around under Hobbs' arm to loose the buttons down the front of Hobbs' coat. Then he snaked a hand in to undo the thong tying Hobbs' holster to his thigh. He worked the gunbelt's buckle till he had it loose, then stepped back to let belt and holster both fall to the ground. He could hear Hobbs' breathing coming harsh and quick, like maybe Hobbs was afraid to draw a deep breath.

"Now we're going in the house. If there's anybody likely to get trigger-happy, you better call out to 'em first chance you get, let 'em know the fix you're in. Anything happens to me, your whole head's going sky-high."

"I don't..." Hobbs looked about to go up on tiptoe, stretching away from those twin muzzles leeched to his throat. "I don't... believe I could. Not like this."

"Don't worry about it. I'll do it myself. One thing before we go in: suppose you tell me where Quinn and Walker are."

"They're in the bunkhouse. They bed down out there."

Slocum tugged gently on the shotgun, bringing Hobbs' head around, pulling him away from the stall. "Don't lie to me, Hobbs. I happen to know they're in the house. You're in a bad position to be testing my patience."

Hobbs eyed him from that rigid stance, head cocked awkwardly up and a little to the side so he had to slant his eyes down just to see. Even with a shotgun lashed to his jaw, there was defiance in his look. "They're in the house."

"Which floor?"

"Second floor. They're sharing a room up there."

"You better hope that's where they are," Slocum said. "Let's go look." He tugged on the Greener again, brought Hobbs around, and nudged him toward the doors.

The sky was a crystal-clear blue outside. The sun was reflecting brilliantly off the white of the snow, but the air was so cold it was brittle. He turned Hobbs left into a narrow path shoveled through the snow toward the house, staying behind him, moving slow. The path had been shoveled clean, but the ground underfoot was solid ice; he could feel his boots threatening to slip with every step. He kept his eyes on the verandas of the house and the single low building where the crew bunked. Smoke rose from a tin chimney pipe above the bunkhouse, but he saw no other sign of life there. Then they moved into the shadow of the house and he saw a face flash out of sight in what he took to be a kitchen window. He took his fingers off the shotgun's triggers and let the weight of his arm pull Hobbs to a stop.

"Somebody just saw us. From that window off the veranda there. Whoever it is, you better be ready to call them off."

"Take this thing off me," Hobbs said. "I can't do nothing like this."

Now a door burst open at the far end of the veranda. Hobbs flinched, but Slocum held him steady. He saw a man swing around the corner of the door, drawing down on him with a Winchester .44 carbine, and now another man appeared behind the first, also with a carbine, both of them holding on him.

The first man jacked a round into his carbine. "You better drop the shotgun, stranger."

Slocum tugged on the Greener. "Call him off."

"Do your own dirty work," Hobbs growled. "You got yourself in here. Get yourself out."

Slocum recognized the second of the two men as David Hobbs, the redhead he'd had the run-in with in Bushnell's. He figured the other was an older son. Now he saw men spilling out of the bunkhouse, a good half-dozen of them, all carrying weapons, coming at a run.

He shifted the Greener to his left hand and drew his Colt. "Red? You remember me, Red. You know who I'm after. You better call your dogs off. I'm set to kill your daddy here if I don't get what I come for."

He saw the first man say something over his shoulder to the redhead, but he was too far away to hear what it was. The men from the bunkhouse had skidded to a stop at the edge of the yard when they saw the shotgun.

He twisted Hobbs' head around to give them a good look at the noose. "I got my fingers on the triggers. Anything happens to me, both barrels go off. It'll kill him even as I'm falling. You better do as I say."

He watched the two Hobbs brothers conferring on the veranda. Now the older one turned to shout at the crew, waving them back toward the bunkhouse. He watched till he was sure they were going, then he turned back to Slocum, studying that shotgun lashed to his daddy's chin. Finally he thumbed down the hammer on the carbine and tossed the carbine out in the snow. When the redhead had done the same, Slocum prodded Hobbs and eased him on along the path to the steps.

The older son was glaring at him. "You be careful, damn it. You could kill him just by accident." To the redhead, he said, "Go tell those men to stay in the bunkhouse. I'll handle this. You all right, Daddy?"

"I'm all right," Hobbs said. "Just don't nobody get hotheaded and careless."

"You send somebody to bring Walker and Quinn down here," Slocum said. "That way I won't have to bother you."

"Find them yourself," Hobbs said. "You'll get no help from me."

"If that's the way you want to play it. Let's go up those steps. Real easy, now."

The son backed up into the doorway. Slocum pushed Hobbs in after him, moving into some sort of dark hallway, wary and watchful. They eased up on a door branching off on the right, into what looked to be a dining room, where he could see a good dozen plates already set around a big table. He could smell breakfast cooking from somewhere deeper in the house. He nudged Hobbs on past the door, the son backing away in front of them, and now the hallway opened out into a big sitting room, with a huge fireplace in the opposite wall and a wide staircase starting up on the right and bending to climb the wall to the second story. He heard footsteps hurrying along an upstairs hall, moving toward the stairs, and he tugged Hobbs to a halt.

It was a woman, stout and gray-haired, wearing a long apron, a dish towel in her hands. She stopped at the bend of the stairs, frightened eyes staring at the shotgun, the dish towel clutched at her middle. "Give him what he wants, Walter. You know Frank's not worth it. Give him what he wants and let him go."

"Shut up, Wilma. Get back up there out of the way."

"You come on down here, ma'am," Slocum said. "Let's just keep everybody together. If I can see everybody, I'm less likely to get nervous. And you don't want me to get nervous with this thing."

Movement on his left brought his eyes around. Now he saw another hallway branching left off the sitting room, past the door to another room on either side. There was a man in the door on the right, or a boy, maybe eighteen, and a young woman standing in the hall staring at him, clutching a little girl to her skirts.

The gray-haired woman had come down off the stairs. Slocum waved the Colt at her, to bring her over beside her son, and tugged on the shotgun again.

"Let's back up along this hall. We're going to take a look in those rooms. If there's anybody there might get careless, you better let them know what's happening."

"There's nobody there but women and kids," Hobbs said. "You want Walker and Quinn, I told you, they're upstairs."

"That's all right. I'll just take a look."

Slowly, head cocked so he could see both the stairs and the young woman behind him, he pulled Hobbs back along the hall till he could see in through the doors. The boy had retreated back into his room and was watching him from behind a chest of drawers, eyes as wide as an owl's. The woman had taken the girl into the room opposite and was sitting on the bed there, clutching the girl to her. A younger boy, maybe eight, still in his night clothes, still in bed, was clinging to her hand.

"You satisfied?" Hobbs said.

"So far," Slocum said. He could see a hallway stretching on beyond the other end of the sitting room, toward what was likely the kitchen. "Let's go take a look down there."

He was beginning not to like this. Too much house

to search, too many people in the way, too many things to worry about. Halfway through the sitting room, he turned Hobbs around and started backing toward the kitchen. The redhead was back from the bunkhouse, glaring at him, following along with his brother. The stout woman, Wilma, was following, too, still clutching the dish towel, worried eyes on the shotgun. The younger woman and the older boy had come out of the rooms he'd just searched and joined the rest, drawn wide-eyed after him. Crowded up in a knot, they followed him along the opposite hallway till he reached the end of it, where he could get a look in through the doors there.

Kitchen on the left. A pantry. Another bedroom, empty. He was out of sight of the stairs, but he would be able to see anybody descending into the sitting room. He was listening hard, but he could hear no sounds from upstairs. That didn't make him feel any better. Still possible there was a way out he couldn't see.

"All right," he said. "Now the stairs. Maybe you better send somebody up first. Just kind of gently disarm those boys. You may be kin to Walker, but not to Quinn. They may not care whether killing me gets you killed, too."

The older son was watching him, quiet but wary. "They wouldn't dare. The man that gets Walter Hobbs killed dies the next instant. You remember that."

"I'll worry about my neck," Hobbs said. "You started this. You play it out."

"All right," Slocum said. "Let's go upstairs."

The little crowd stayed with him into the sitting room, but only the two Hobbs boys started up the stairs with him. The rest collected in a knot at the

foot of the staircase, the gray-haired woman holding
the dish towel clutched to her mouth, all of them
staring after him. The ceiling of the sitting room
reached all the way to the rafters. He could see the
staircase opened onto a hall running the length of the
house, only the stretch above the sitting room visible
through a railing. There would be doors he couldn't
see on both the left and the right. And neither Walker
nor Quinn might care about killing any Hobbs—father
*or* sons—if they thought they could shoot their way
clear.

He prodded Hobbs on up to the top of the stairs,
the sons following close behind. One door directly
across from him. One each in the same wall farther
down on the left and the right. Two more doors opening off the hall opposite them. And all the doors closed.

He waved the older son up and pointed his Colt
at the door straight in front of him. "Open it."

The son slipped past him, took a look both ways
along the hall, and opened the door. Slocum pushed
Hobbs across the hall and took a look inside.

Another young woman sat on the edge of a bed in
the near corner, holding the hand of a man swathed
in bandages, his eyes closed, his breathing ragged. A
chamber pot was just visible under the bed. Slocum
saw a lamp on the table near the window, and he
realized he was in the bedroom he had seen that lamp
come to rest in all those mornings he'd watched the
house from the ridge on the west. The young woman
was looking defiantly at him, frightened but determined.

"That's my son," Hobbs said. "You've seen him.
Now leave him alone."

"I ain't going to touch him," Slocum said. "You

know that. You just take me to the right room, and this'll be over."

And then he saw movement out on the snow beyond the window. He didn't have to move to the window to see what it was: two horses, two riders, crossing the snow at a run, already halfway to the hills.

The two Hobbs brothers were watching him. He could tell by the set of Hobbs' shoulders that the old man too knew he had seen them and was braced against whatever was coming next. Wherever Quinn and Walker had come from—out of some door he hadn't seen, or maybe jumping off this second-story veranda—it didn't matter. All he could do was watch them go.

He looked to the redhead. "All right," he said. "You gave them their chance. You paid off any debt you owe to Walker. Now I'll tell you what we're going to do. We're going to go out in the barn, and you're going to saddle me a horse. I figure getting your old man here on a horse with this scattergun lashed to his chin is too risky, so we'll just take one horse, in case they find mine up there. I'm going to take your daddy with me. Anybody follows, I'm going to kill him. When I get up on that ridge, I'll let him go. And you better hope Walker cares as much about his Uncle Walter as his Uncle Walter cared about him. I get shot crossing that snow, Walter Hobbs is going to die. Everybody clear?"

The redhead looked to his brother. The brother shrugged. "You're calling the shots."

"All right, then. Now we go back down the stairs. Nice and easy."

He figured it took him an hour to cross the Pocket to the ridge on the west. He had to walk the horse the redhead had saddled for him; either Walker or Quinn had taken the roan he'd left in the stall in the barn. He pushed Hobbs on ahead with the shotgun, trying to keep the old man in front of him, watching the timber up on that ridge. He made about as good a target as those two up there could want. But either they were waiting till he turned Hobbs loose or they had decided to put as much ground behind them as possible. He made it up into the trees without mishap.

The tracks led on up through the timber. He saw a churned-up place in the snow where they had turned to take a look back, then more tracks disappearing on up the ridge. He turned Hobbs around so he could see back across the Pocket.

The crew was back out of the bunkhouse, gathered along the edge of the yard, watching. The crowd from the house was clustered along the veranda railing, the two sons standing beside the woman wearing the apron. So far nobody was making a move to follow him.

He eased the slip knot loose from the Greener and pulled it off over Hobbs' head. Hobbs cricked his neck and rubbed at his jaw, eyeing the shotgun as Slocum propped it against a tree.

Slocum tapped the butt of his Colt. "Don't try it. You're an old man. You'd never make it." He uncoiled the rope from his saddle horn, working out a loop.

"Thought you were going to let me go," Hobbs said.

"I ain't letting you go, but I'll leave you here. Time those boys get up nerve to come take a look, I'll be long gone."

He swung the loop over Hobbs' shoulders and pulled it tight, cinching the man's arms tight to his sides.

Then he backed him up against a tree and started winding the rope around both Hobbs and the tree trunk. He could hear Hobbs' breath coming loud and harsh—likely all this had put a strain on the old man—but there were no sounds from up the hill. He hoped those two had decided to make a good run for it while they had the chance.

"You better think hard on what it is you're going to do when those sons of yours set you loose," he said. "You send anybody after me, they'll come along. You know it. You couldn't stop them. If it comes to that, you're going to lose another son or two. I guarantee it."

Hobbs just stared off into the distance, sullen, not saying anything.

"You know Frank Walker's not worth risking your sons on," Slocum said. "How close did he come to telling you the truth? He tell you how him and them others pulled my woman naked out of her bath and raped her? He tell you they left her lying there with a knife in her belly for me to come home and find? Your nephew's an animal, Hobbs. You know he ain't worth risking your sons on."

Hobbs still didn't say anything. Slocum tied the rope around his ankles and cut it off with his knife. Then he unloaded the shotgun, slung it from the saddlehorn, and mounted up. He could see that crowd still clustered around the house. So far, so good. He kicked the horse in the ribs and headed around the side of the hill, toward where he had left the bay.

The bay was waiting patiently where he'd left it. He switched horses, lashed the Greener on back of the saddle, and kicked the bay up into the timber. A hundred yards above where he'd left Hobbs he found

the tracks again, climbing due west, heading toward
Chilly Wind Pass. He loosened the Winchester in its
saddle boot and started up after them.

# 18

He tracked them all that day and all through the next and on through the night that followed.

The rough country wouldn't let him move as fast as he wanted, but he kept the bay working steadily up through the timber, jumping felled trees and lunging up over rocky outcrops and spurring into a trot whenever the ground levelled out on the crest of a ridge. By mid-afternoon of the first day he could hear the horse already laboring for air, lungs heaving under his knees like a bellows working to keep a forge fire hot, and he had to let up some and slow the pace for a stretch. He didn't like to ride a horse that hard, but he had a good idea how much it could take and how long it would last, and his impatience wouldn't let him slow up long.

Toward late afternoon the sky clouded over and it began to snow, a fine powdery snow blowing through the treetops. Soon it was snowing in earnest, closing down on him fast, a sudden squall that left him blind for as long as an hour, hunkered up in the lee of a narrow little ridge and waiting impatiently for it to pass so he could set out up the mountain again. He knew the snow was blotting out their tracks, but he didn't need tracks to follow. So long as they were on this side of Chilly Wind, he knew where they were headed. Let them cross the pass and start down the

other side, though, and he would lose them. Without
tracks to follow there, they had half the country to
lose themselves in. It might take him months to find
a trace of them again. As soon as the snow let up
enough for him to see a little, he was in the saddle
again, urging the bay on, up into that high country,
climbing all the time and straining to find some sign
of them ahead.

He rode on into the dusk till he could no longer
see even by the light coming off the snow. He pulled
down into a narrow little draw then, put the nosebag
on the bay, and fixed himself a spot for his bedroll
under the branches of a downed tree. He ate some of
the meat and bread Susan had fixed, washing it down
with water from his canteen, and curled up in his
blankets, unable to make a fire for fear it would be
seen.

Despite an hour of tossing in his blankets, he
couldn't sleep. He had to fight off an uneasy feeling
that Walker and Quinn might not be bedding down at
all, that Walker might know the country well enough
to ride on in the dark, slower maybe but still moving,
putting more ground behind them all the time. Then
he recognized that thought for what it was, just something for his impatience to chew on, and he tried to
put his mind on something else, and that left him
thinking about Susan. It was the first night he had
spent in weeks without the certain knowledge he could
have her next to him when he wanted, and it left him
itchy and lonely and wondering if he had done the
right thing telling her he wanted her on that wagon
out; and then he knew he couldn't think about her,
either, and he turned in his blankets again and tried
to blank out his mind the way he had in Hobbs' barn.

He was eager for dawn, eager to be up and moving again, heading after Walker and Quinn.

It was near noon of the second day before he caught his first sight of them. The snow had stopped and the sky had cleared, stretching an unbroken blue overhead. He was up in high country now, the air as dry and cold as any he'd ever breathed. For close to an hour he had been riding along the spine of a sparsely timbered ridge, sunlight reflecting through the trees, and then he climbed up out of the timber and saw the deep cut of Chilly Wind Pass etched against the blue of the sky up ahead. He figured it was still twenty miles away, a vast expanse of snow climbing up above the timberline, giving way to abrupt gray cliffs thrusting up toward that blue and brittle sky; and then his eyes adjusted to the distance and he saw two small dots barely visible on the wide trough of snow between the cliffs, and he knew it was them. He reined the bay up short, brought the field glasses out of his saddlebags, and pulled those two tiny dots into focus.

They were too far away to see clear, even with the glasses, but he could tell it was them. They were moving across a wide, steep slope on the left edge of the pass, the snow so deep the horses looked to be swimming. He watched them for close to five minutes, trying to tell Walker from Quinn, the old poison fuming in his gut like something in a slaughterhouse vat, the glasses making them seem close, even small as they were, so that he felt he could reach out and pluck them off that snow like ants off a leaf.

Likely they felt they were safe now. They would figure Hobbs had at least slowed him down enough to let them get away—fast enough and far enough so he couldn't catch up to them. They would think all they had to contend with now was the snow and the cold and the mountains. He was looking forward to teaching them different.

And then he calculated how long it would take them to make it on through the pass and how far he was behind them, and he stashed the glasses and kicked the bay into a trot. At the rate he had been moving, they would be through the pass and started down the other side before he could hope to catch up to them. And he couldn't let that happen.

The sun set behind those towering cliffs and he rode on into the twilight. Then the twilight became dusk, and the dusk became night, and he rode on into the dark till the dark itself drove him down out of the saddle and he continued on afoot, leading the bay, guided solely by the starlight reflecting off the snow. Soon the moon rose on the horizon to the east, casting spidery shadows down through the trees. Then the sky began to haze over, and the moon began drifting behind clouds, and then the sky was dark again, with only an occasional patch of stars glittering through to light the way.

By midnight he had long since ceased to feel much at all. He was moving by instinct now, driven by that mindless energy that had kept him on the trail all the way from Texas, not faltering even when sleep threatened to lay him low, pushing on into the night with only one thought burning in his brain: if he kept moving all night, without stopping even once to rest, then he might reach their camp by daybreak and catch them still in their beds.

Trees loomed out of the night at him. Once he walked straight into a low-hanging limb he hadn't even seen. He fell several times in the snow, and once his feet went out from under him along the edge of a deep ravine, and only the fact that he held to the reins and the bay stood fast kept him from sliding down a snowy slope so steep likely hitting the bottom would have killed him. A deer spooked out of some brush shortly after midnight, and twice he startled what he could tell by the sounds was a bear. Once he actually saw the bear rise up in what little light there was, not twenty feet in front of him, huge and black against the dim white of the snow, and then it dipped and faded out of sight in the dark, crashing down through the timber of a draw falling away to his left, and he calmed the nervous horse and moved on.

Long before dawn, he was so tired he could barely continue. His brain was a fog from lack of sleep. Soon the timber fell away behind him, and he knew he was above the timberline, and then he sensed those huge gray cliffs dwarfing him on either side and he knew he was in the pass, in Chilly Wind, on that vast trough of snow he had sighted Walker and Quinn on that afternoon. That stirred new life in him; he seemed to come awake, sensing he was closing in on them, sleep fading from him like something in a dream. The first faint tint of gray began to light the sky behind him, the day dawning gray and cloudy. He mounted up then and moved down out of the pass into the timber on the other side.

He was riding along the crest of a ridge, in dense pines, when he caught a whiff of smoke. He hauled back on the reins and like a bear himself raised his nose to the wind and sniffed. He was so high up the clouds hung in the trees like fog; if there was smoke in the air, he couldn't see it. And then he smelled it again, coming from somewhere up ahead and to the right of him. He brought the Winchester up out of the saddle boot and nudged the bay on into the pines.

He had gone maybe thirty yards when he saw movement through the trees. He pulled the bay abruptly to a halt, holding it steady while he searched the terrain ahead of him. All he could see was tree trunks and tree limbs and black clumps of brush against the snow. He swung down out of the saddle and tied the bay to a tree and moved on afoot, in a crouch now, watching for movement.

They were already saddled up, ready to ride out. He crouched down behind a tree trunk, watching them move around a dying campfire. The snow around the fire showed where they had laid their bedrolls, but the bedrolls were already lashed on back of their saddles, and Walker was kicking at the coals of the fire, scattering them on the snow. Quinn held the horses just beyond the fire, waiting. He said something to Walker, and Slocum saw Walker grin and turn back toward the horses.

He felt that vicious heat flare up inside and beat against the back of his eyes, and he brought the Winchester around and laid the sights of it on Walker's back and tried to steady himself, forced that heat down till the rifle barrel stopped trembling.

Walker had taken the reins of his horse. Quinn had his stirrup reversed and was preparing to mount. Slocum jacked a round into the chamber, the sound so loud it brought the horses' heads up.

*"Walker? Quinn?"*

Walker wheeled, jerking his rifle out of the saddle boot. Slocum shot him and saw him drop and swung the Winchester toward Quinn. Quinn's horse had tried to bolt, and Quinn was hanging on to the reins, trying to fight it to a standstill so he could mount, but now Walker's sorrel squealed and lashed out at him with a front hoof, sunfishing around like a bronc in a tight corral. Quinn had to duck under its lashing hooves, fighting his own mount all the while, but he got hold of his saddlehorn and tried to drag himself up. Slocum fired again and hit the sorrel and saw its left hind leg buckle as it went limping off into the trees. And then Quinn was up in the saddle and kicking his mount into a run, heading for a little trail running along the spine of the ridge beyond the far end of the campsite. Slocum sent a bullet after him and saw the horse falter and stumble and go down, skidding in the snow, sending Quinn head over heels out of sight down a steep bank off to the right of the trail.

Slocum looked just long enough to be sure Walker was dead. Then he cut right at a run, dodging tree limbs, and vaulted down over that bank himself.

# 19

His boots went out from under him and he skidded
ten yards on his backside. He came up already running, levering another round into the chamber, aiming
for the place he'd seen Quinn go down. When he saw
the dark bulk of the horse in the snow up ahead, he
went down on his belly and crawled up behind a pine
where he could see.

The horse had slid down off the trail into a little
clearing. The clearing stretched the length of a shallow
ravine between two little rises of ground sloping like
ribs down off the spine of the ridge. The horse lay
on its side, not moving, blood soaking the snow around
it. He could see the rifle was gone from its scabbard.
A set of boot tracks led across the clearing into the
trees on the other side.

He lay on his belly in the snow, watching those
trees, listening. His breath rose white in front of his
face. There wasn't a sound for miles, not even a breeze
in the trees. He had hit the horse, but he didn't think
he had hit Quinn; there was no blood in those boot
tracks. Likely Quinn was lying on his belly, too,
watching the treeline same as he was. He wanted to
know where.

"Quinn?" He waited, hoping to draw a shot. "Paul,
you over there?"

Nothing. He eased up behind the tree till he was

173

standing, sure that Quinn would see the movement if
he was watching.

"Paul? You're the last one left, Paul."

No answer. Not even a sign of movement.

"I killed Foley before he even got out of Coffey,
Paul. I guess you know I killed Charley. I come back
to get you."

Nothing. Quinn was too smart to try a chancy shot.
Or maybe he wasn't watching; maybe he had left his
position and was moving, looking for a better one.
Slocum could see a clear spot where the trail passed
along above that patch of trees over there. If Quinn
had moved, it couldn't have been uphill or he would
have seen him. Could be he was working his way
down through the timber, hoping to circle around and
come up behind him. That was all right. Let Quinn
move downhill. He would move up and take the high
ground on him.

He crawled backward till the rise of ground put the
clearing out of sight, then rose to a crouch and worked
his way back up across the spine of the ridge. He
skirted around the blackened campfire, where Walker
lay sprawled in the blood-soaked snow, and moved
on west along the ridge. He came up on Walker's
sorrel, spooked it, and watched it hobble on another
twenty yards and come to a halt again. The sleepless
fog had left him. He felt as clear-brained and wide-
awake as he'd been any time since leaving Jackson
County. When he figured he was even with the timber
Quinn had taken shelter in, he crossed the trail and
dodged down off the ridge into the trees.

This time he sheltered behind a tree where he could
see across the shallow ravine to the place he had just
left. Nothing had changed. The snow was still un-

marked save for that single line of boot tracks. From down the hill a ways he heard the thump of a hare, carried to him through the hushed morning quiet, but that was the only sound. He rose to a crouch again and started easing down the slope, moving from tree to tree.

The sudden snap of a tree limb brought him up sharp. Somewhere down below him, maybe forty yards. Could have been a tree cracking with the cold. Or a downed limb being stepped on. He waited, one shoulder edged up against the trunk of a large pine, watching, listening. When he heard nothing else, he left the shelter of the pine and started on down through the snow.

Then he heard another tree limb snap. He stopped where he was, rifle held across his middle, listening again. Silence. Could have been the cold. Quinn had no real reason to move. All he had to do was wait, let things come to him. A man who was being stalked had the advantage; the man doing the stalking had to make noise, noise that would give away where he was.

Now a sudden movement in the trees below him brought the rifle up. Something dark, moving across his line of sight toward the clearing. He lost it, saw it move again and then stop again. Then he saw it was a deer, a buck, standing in the trees at the edge of the clearing, with a rack the size of an upturned rocking chair on its head. The buck stood motionless for a moment; then it seemed to sense him watching and bounded off down through the timber in swift and almost soundless flight. He lowered the rifle and moved on.

Twenty yards down the slope he came on the boot

tracks where Quinn had entered the trees. A blurred
patch of snow showed where he had turned and hunkered down, watching his back trail. From the look of
things he hadn't stayed there long; another set of boot
prints led away down through the timber—the deep-
dug, wide-spaced prints of a man moving at a run.

Slocum scanned the trees ahead of him, wondering
why Quinn had been in such a hurry. Quinn's best
bet was to lay up somewhere and wait for him, and
the place where he had been, with that clear view
across the clearing, was as good as any. Quinn didn't
know this country, and a man being stalked didn't
move that fast and careless unless he had some par-
ticular place in mind. And then he knew where Quinn
was headed. Likely he had seen that sorrel lamed. His
own horse was dead. Two men high up in the mountains in the cold of winter, and only one horse to carry
either of them out. Quinn was after the bay.

That was all right. That was even better. Let Quinn
come to him. He turned and started working his way
back up the slope.

He found the bay where he had left it, tied to a
pine near the east edge of the campsite Quinn and
Walker had picked out the night before. Skirting around
the campsite, he had run onto the sorrel, down on its
side now, blood draining into the snow. The sorrel
struggled up when he passed it, hobbled a yard or
two, and then went down again; he could see the left
hind knee joint was shattered. He slanted down the
south side of the ridge and circled around, coming up
into thick brush along the crest, with the bay ahead
and maybe a dozen yards to the right of him.

The ridge was only forty yards wide here. The
timber was sparse along the crest, where the horse

was, but dense on the slopes falling away on either side. Quinn should be coming up through the pines on the north. Slocum hunkered down in the brush, reloading the Winchester. He could see through the brush, right up in it like he was, but Quinn wouldn't be able to make him out from forty yards away. He set himself to wait, watching the treeline on the other side.

He heard Quinn before he saw him: slow, faint footfalls coming up through the snow. Quinn may have started off at a run, but he was moving carefully now; if he hadn't been listening for it, he would never have heard it. He shifted his Winchester a little to the left, holding on where he figured Quinn would appear.

For a long while nothing happened. The footfalls had stopped. The bay shifted and stirred off to his right, mouthing its bit, but that was the only sound. He figured Quinn had halted someplace where he could watch the bay and was waiting till he was sure the coast was clear. He held himself still and tried not to breathe.

Something moved in the treeline. He saw the barrel of a rifle slant around the trunk of a tree—Quinn easing just enough of his head around to get a look. He watched Quinn's eyes checking out the trees, scanning the terrain in back of the bay, then moving back to do the same thing all over again. Quinn stayed where he was for more than a minute. Then he stepped out from behind the tree, facing the horse, watching, waiting.

He was carrying the rifle in one hand and had his Colt in the other. His sheepskin was open down the front and his hat hung by a cord down his back. He stood there for a moment—short, stocky, head up like that buck down there sniffing the wind. When he was satisfied, he stepped out of the treeline and started toward the bay.

Slocum rose out of the brush, Winchester levelled on Quinn's chest. "I wouldn't advise it."

Quinn halted where he was. He had been fumbling at his sheepskin, moving to holster his Colt so he could mount the bay, and his rifle was slanting toward the ground. Now he stopped dead, head cocked to one side, and something as strange as a smile crossed his face.

"And all the time I thought it was me being smart," he said.

"You was smart, you wouldn't have been here in the first place."

"You had your nose to the trail so many months, I figured you'd follow them tracks like a bloodhound." Quinn looked at the Colt in his hand, shrugged, and tossed it casually off into the snow. He dropped the Winchester at his feet and kicked it over toward the Colt. "Well, you got me cold. Now what are you going to do with me?"

"Going to kill you as soon as you tell me what I want to know."

The old easy grin spread Quinn's face. "No, you ain't. I know you, John. You won't shoot a man that can't shoot back."

"I wouldn't count on it."

"Oh, I'd bet money on it. I ain't so foolish as to draw on you. You can maybe prod Charley Beaumont into drawing on you, or Bob Foley, but you can't prod me."

Slocum stayed where he was. "I already heard Beaumont and Foley. Suppose you tell me your version of it. Maybe you can tell me why you would treat a woman like you did."

That easy grin again. "She was a good-looking woman, John. You take a look at me, now. You can see I'm a Mex, can't you? Half Mex. Same thing. She wouldn't have looked at me any other way."

"Talk straight. I want to know what happened."

Quinn shrugged. "We was drunk, John, You know the things a man will do when he's drunk."

"There's some things some men won't do even drunk. I thought you were one of them."

"Yeah, you always fancied you knew me. You didn't know nothing. That wouldn't have been the first time I had a woman didn't want to have me. How else is a Mex like me even going to lay a hand on a white woman?"

"Tell me what happened, Paul. Then you can pick up a gun."

"No, John, you got to take me back to Texas to stand trial. That's a long ways. A long ways for one man to guard another." He grinned. "Maybe you won't make it all the way to Texas."

"You ain't going to make it off this mountain. Who killed her, Paul?"

Quinn shrugged. "What difference does it make? You already killed Bob Foley for it. You killed Charley Beaumont for it, and Charley wasn't even there when it happened."

"Who killed her, Paul?"

"What good will it do you? She's dead, John."

"I want to know which of my friends was animal enough to kill my woman."

"You calling me an animal, John?"

"It was an animal pulled her out of that tub. Whoever

killed her's worse than an animal."

Quinn began to flush, sullen and angry. "You think it was me?"

"You go ahead and tell me."

"You think it was me? Think it was the Mex did it?"

"I want to hear you say it."

"You think it was me?" Quinn shrugged. "Sure, it was me. Why not? She was after me with a knife. She would have killed me. She snatched that knife off a sideboard when Frank let go of her. It was going to be my turn, you see. Old Pablito's turn. Give the Mex a shot at her. That's the way it always was, wasn't it? The Mex always sucking hind tit. Frank has her, and then when it's my turn she's got a knife. Oh, I didn't aim to do it. I was just wrestling with her. Trying to get the knife away. All that wrestling around, she got the knife in her belly. You think I wanted that? Hell, what good's a dead woman to me? I wanted what the others had."

Slocum felt his insides go dead cold, ice threatening to frost over his eyes. "Pick up a gun, Paul."

"No, John, you got to take me back to Texas. If you can get that far with me."

"Pick up a gun, Paul."

Quinn shook his head. "You're making a fuss over a little thing. She was just a woman, John. She was just another woman."

Slocum shot him.

The bullet took Quinn in the arm, right above the elbow. The shock of it brought a strangled cry from his throat, and he grabbed at his arm, going down almost to one knee before he caught himself. He stared at the blood seeping through his fingers, blinking like a dull-witted man trying to get something difficult through his mind.

Slocum jacked another round into the chamber. "Pick up a gun, Paul."

Quinn stared at him, mouth agape, eyes blinking with that arduous effort to understand just what was happening. He swallowed once, like maybe he was going to say something, and then he looked back down at his arm as if he couldn't believe what he'd seen there.

Slocum shot him in the other arm.

Quinn jerked, that stunned and strangled gasp coming from his throat again, a note of shocked surprise in it, like the whine of a kid protesting unjust punishment. This time he went all the way to his knees, still holding one arm, blinking stupidly at the blood coming from the other. He shook his head, as if to make this bad dream go away, and turned those blinking eyes back toward Slocum.

"Better pick up a gun, Paul. This keeps on, you won't be able to hold one."

Quinn just stared at him. Slocum jacked another round into the chamber and raised the rifle again.

Quinn blinked once and dived to his left, landing on his belly and scrambling to his knees, scuttling toward that Colt he'd tossed away. Slocum took careful aim and fired at the Colt, hitting it, sending it spinning just out of reach across the snow. A little whine of protest came from Quinn's throat again, and he lunged for the Colt, seized it, rolled onto his back and wheeled up on his knees. He was bringing the Colt around in both hands when Slocum shot him in the belly.

Quinn jumped a little, but he stayed on his knees.

Head bowed, he sagged slowly, the hands clasped around the Colt sinking toward his chest like maybe he had decided it was time to pray. Then his head bent all the way down, as if he had changed his mind and decided now he wanted a careful look at the hole in his belly. The Colt went all the way down into the snow, and his weight came forward on his hands and rested there. And Slocum shot him again.

This time the shot blew Quinn over onto his back, one leg canted awkwardly up underneath him. He jerked once, twice, spasmodically, and lay still.

Slocum crossed to the bay and stuck the Winchester in the saddle boot. Then he untied the reins and began leading the bay back toward where he'd seen the sorrel. He had just put one animal out of its misery. He figured he would go put the other one out of its misery, too.

# 20

It took him two days to get back down out of the mountains. He reached the hills above Hobbs' Pocket just at dusk and stopped there long enough to roll himself a smoke and watch all the lamps being lit in the house. He had seen no sign Hobbs had sent any men after him. Could be they had made a stab at it and then turned back and the snow had blown over their tracks, but he didn't think so. If Hobbs had wanted him bad enough, they wouldn't have turned back. No, he figured Hobbs had written Walker off. Blood was thicker than water, they said, but there was such a thing as bad blood, too. Hobbs was trying to convince himself the blood he had passed on was good.

Slocum wondered if that oldest son had died. He watched for a long time, but no lamp was lit in the upstairs bedroom. Could be Hobbs had had something more pressing on his mind than Frank Walker. He watched a while longer, then turned the bay back into the trees and headed south down out of the hills.

On the southern rim of the Hole he hooked up with the trail that ran on out toward the road to Coffey. The trail took him around near the draw Tom Price's cabin was in, but he rode on past the turn-off that would have taken him there. He didn't want to face the questions Ganning and Price would want answers to, and he didn't want to hear the answer to the one question still in his own mind. They would know whether Susan had caught that ride out to Coffey with Bushnell's cook, and he didn't want to think about that till he had to.

It was long after dark by the time he reached the road to Coffey. Bushnell's windows were showing lights when he passed it on the ridge to the east, but he was already looking for lamplight in the hills ahead of him, knowing he had no right to expect any there, holding his mind down tight against what it would mean if he didn't—and what it would mean if he did. He hadn't expected to feel this way. Only when he'd started down out of Chilly Wind had he realized that feeling had been sitting in his gut all the time.

He dipped down out of the trees and crossed the road and started up through the trees on the other side. The sky was clear, stretching like black ice from horizon to horizon; the night seemed to crackle with the cold. In the light of a quarter-moon he could see a horse had broken trail through the snow no later than that afternoon, and he flicked the bay with his spurs, a little spasm of anticipation squirming through his gut. He wouldn't let himself admit what that was about, but he had a sudden clear memory of the night he had come up through these pines and found her sitting there in the shack, bundled up in that bulky coat, her cracked high-topped shoes peeking out from under her dress, her two bundles resting on the floor at her feet. It cost him an effort not to think about what he might find when he got there this time.

He started up the last rise, and now even the bay pricked up its ears, maybe catching scent of what smelled like home. When he crested the rise, he came out on ground blown almost bare by the wind, the bay's hooves cracking ice where an earlier rain had filled hoofprints left there before the last freeze, and then he came up out of the trees onto level ground and saw lamplight glowing through the skins over the windows of the shack, and he kicked the bay into a trot, trying to hold down that stir of anticipation tightening up his gut.

He rode on past the door and dismounted. The bay whickered once, and an answering nicker came from the woodshed, where he'd left the packhorse he'd told Susan to sell in Coffey. He loosened the saddle cinch— time enough to unsaddle later—and led the bay toward the shed. And then he saw there were two horses stalled there, and that neither of them was the packhorse he'd left for Susan.

Now he saw another horse on a picket rope off in the dark, barely visible in the starlight, and a pack-saddle he didn't recognize stashed against an outside wall. Not letting himself think, he turned to see that somebody had doused the lamp inside. The shack was as dark as the night around him.

Then a voice came from somewhere near the door, a man's voice, trying not to sound scared. "Who is it out there? Come on, if you're friendly. I got a gun on you if you're not."

The man must have heard him coming up the hill. He could barely make him out, a vague form half-shielded by the open door. He killed the last of the anticipation already dwindling in his belly and held his hands out away from his sides to show he had nothing in them.

"Didn't mean to put a scare into you. Didn't know anybody was in there. I been holing up in this shack. Should be some of my gear still in there."

"Come on over where I can see you," the man said. "Careful-like."

Slocum left the shed and moved toward the door, still holding his hands out. When he got close he could see the man had a rifle on him, a Winchester, holding steady on his gut.

"You got nothing to worry about from me," he said. "I'm heading out. Been away a couple days, but I'm heading out now for good. Just wanted to pick up my gear."

"You got anybody with you?"

"I'm alone. You can see my horse there. I got no use for this place anymore. Just let me get my gear, and I'll leave you to it."

The man said something to somebody inside, and Slocum heard whoever it was strike a match. A glow of light widened in the door as a lamp was lit behind it. The man lowered the rifle and waved him on in.

There was a woman inside, a spare lean woman with her hair tied back in a bun, her face showing strain that had been there long before she'd heard him ride up outside. She was standing by the table, turning up the wick of a lamp. It was the same lamp Susan had got from Tom Price, but the bear robe Price had given her was gone from the bed, along with the featherbed and her bedroll and the bundle she'd brought with her from Bushnell's. The floor now was strewn with what these two had been packing—bundles scattered half-opened all around the room. They couldn't have been here more than a few hours.

The man was still carrying the Winchester, but he had it pointed at the floor now. "Sorry for the welcome," he said. "Didn't know anybody was using this place first off. Time we seen your gear, it was dark out there. We was lost, tell the truth. We was just glad to find shelter."

"Well, now you got a place to spend the winter in," Slocum said. "I'm putting Hobbs' Hole behind me."

The woman roped her gnarled hands together and flicked a glance toward her man. "Don't mean to put you out," she said. "Maybe he could throw a bedroll down, Wendell. Spend the night, and then leave in the morning."

Slocum could tell by the look on his face that didn't set too well with Wendell. "No need for that. Won't be the first time I made a night ride. And I'm used to sleeping out in the weather."

"Better let me cook you up some supper first." Again she flicked that glance toward her man, pressing on with what she seemed to know wasn't going to meet with his approval. "I can put something on the fire. I was just fixing to."

"I got a stop to make before I ride out," Slocum said. "Place down in the south corner of the Hole. I can get something there."

"You go ahead and get your gear," the man said. "It's all there. We ain't touched none of it."

Slocum retrieved his bag from its place in the corner and gathered up the rest of his things. It didn't take him but a few minutes. There was only his spare bridle, some extra longjohns, a few odds and ends. When he'd got it together, he looked around the room for anything he might have forgotten, but he had it all, so little he could carry it in one arm. The man was standing by the door, still carrying the Winchester, not saying anything but clearly impatient to see him gone. The woman was watching him, a good month's worth of weariness, maybe more, showing in her face.

She left her place beside the table now and crossed to the opposite wall. "I reckon this is yours," she said. "It was here when we got here."

She held it out to him, the scrap of photograph she had plucked off the mirror, just one thin strip now showing a young Pablito Quinn, bright-eyed and jaunty, wearing wooly chaps and a cartridge belt across his chest, all that black Mexican hair cropped so short the white of his scalp was shining through. And down at one corner, the toe of a boot where the rest of the picture had been torn off.

"I seen it first off," she said. "I figured he was a friend of somebody's. Whoever was sheltering here."

"He was a friend of mine," Slocum said. "An old friend from a long time back. You keep it. Burn it. I got no use for it anymore."

Outside, he tied his gear on behind his bedroll and tightened up the saddle cinch. The man was standing in the doorway, watching him, still carrying the rifle, but the woman had stayed inside. He mounted up and turned the bay and headed down toward the road. When he was a dozen yards past the corner of the shack he saw the light fade in the trees as the door was closed behind him.

Only when he was out of sight and across the road did he let himself think about the rest of the picture, the strip that had himself on it, the part that must be riding now in Susan's pocket, wherever she was, in some bare hotel room somewhere or looking out a window on some cold and lonely train, sensing the barren prairie fleeing past outside, lost in her thoughts same as he was, with nothing but the black of night for company.